"Thank you for hiring me," Irene said softly.

As the bodyguards trailed past him to the rear cabin, Sharif frowned in surprise. "Thank you for solving my problem."

A flight attendant served some sparkling water on a silver tray. Taking a sip of the cool water, Irene looked at her new employer.

Sharif looked handsome and powerful in his stark white robes, sitting on the white leather sofa on the other side of the spacious cabin.

A low laugh escaped her lips. "No one would ever have guessed I'd someday be companion to a princess of Makhtar. Are you still sure about this?"

He set down his glass. His handsome face was inscrutable as he slowly looked her over. "Why wouldn't I be?"

Irene hesitated, feeling self-conscious. "I told you I have a bad habit of talking back to employers. Knowing the kind of woman I am, Your Highness, are you sure you really want me as your employee?"

"I'm sure, Miss Taylor. There can be no doubt." His black eyes met hers as he said huskily, "I want you."

All about the author...
Jennie Lucas

JENNIE LUCAS had a tragic beginning for any would-be writer: a very happy childhood. Her parents owned a bookstore, and she grew up surrounded by books, dreaming about faraway lands. When she was ten, her father secretly paid her a dollar for every classic novel *(Jane Eyre, War and Peace)* that she read.

At fifteen, she went to a Connecticut boarding school on scholarship. She took her first solo trip to Europe at sixteen, then put off college and traveled around the United States, supporting herself with jobs as diverse as gas station cashier and newspaper advertising assistant.

At twenty-two, she met the man who would become her husband. For the first time in her life, she wanted to stay in one place, as long as she could be with him. After their marriage, she graduated from Kent State University with a degree in English, and started writing books a year later.

Jennie was a finalist in the Romance Writers of America's Golden Heart contest in 2003 and won the award in 2005. A fellow 2003 finalist, Australian author Trish Morey, read Jennie's writing and told her that she should write for the Harlequin® Presents line. It seemed like too big a dream, but Jennie took a deep breath and went for it. A year later Jennie got the magical call from London that turned her into a published author.

Since then, life has been hectic, juggling a writing career, a sexy husband and two young children, but Jennie loves her crazy, chaotic life. Now if she can only figure out how to pack up her family and live in all the places she's writing about!

For more about Jennie and her books, please visit her website at www.jennielucas.com.

Other titles by Jennie Lucas available in ebook format:

THE CONSEQUENCES OF THAT NIGHT *(At His Service)*
A REPUTATION FOR REVENGE *(Princes Untamed)*
DEALING HER FINAL CARD *(Princes Untamed)*
TO LOVE, HONOR AND BETRAY

Jennie Lucas

The Sheikh's Last Seduction

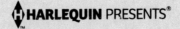

Recycling programs
for this product may
not exist in your area.

ISBN-13: 978-0-373-13701-5

THE SHEIKH'S LAST SEDUCTION

First North American Publication 2014

Copyright © 2014 by Jennie Lucas

Printed in U.S.A.

The Sheikh's Last Seduction

To Pete,

who said "OF COURSE you should go to Dubai!"

Thanks, honey, for giving me the world, every single day.

CHAPTER ONE

HE KNEW HE wanted her from the moment he saw her.

Sharif bin Nazih al-Aktoum, the Emir of Makhtar, had been laughing at the joke of a friend when he turned and saw a woman, standing alone in the Italian moonlight, on the shores of Lake Como.

She stood past a thicket of trees farther down the hill. Her white dress was translucent in the silvery glow of light, and the bare trees of November left latticed shadows like dark lace against her skin. Her black hair cascaded down her shoulders, tumbling, lustrous as onyx. Her eyes were closed in her heart-stoppingly lovely face as her sensual lips whispered unheard words.

Sharif's laughter fled. Was she a ghost? A dream?

Just some wedding guest, he told himself harshly. Nothing special. A trick of moonlight.

And yet…

He stared at her.

Moments before, he'd been chuckling at the poor bridegroom, who'd recently been a famous playboy but had made the mistake of getting his housekeeper pregnant. The new bride was very beautiful, yes, he conceded, and seemed loyal and kind. But still, Sharif would never get caught that way. Not until the bitter end.

Not until—

Sharif pushed the thought away, jerking his chin in the direction of the lakeshore. "Who is that?"

"Who?"

"The woman. By the lake."

His friend, the Duque de Alzacar, craned his head right and left. "I don't see anyone."

Between them and the unknown woman well-dressed wedding guests were milling about the terraces, drinking champagne and enjoying the coolness of the late-autumn night. The intimate evening wedding, held in a medieval chapel on an Italian tycoon's estate, had just ended, and they were waiting for the dinner reception to begin. But surely his friend could see the angel by the lake. "Are you blind?" Sharif said impatiently.

"Describe her to me."

Sharif parted his lips to do just that, then thought better of it. The Spanish duke was the most reckless, irredeemable womanizer he knew—which reminded him of the old saying about the pot and the kettle. But looking back at the soft moonlight on the *houri* by the lake, Sharif felt the sudden strange need to protect her, even from another man's glance. She seemed from another world. Sensual, magical—pure…

"Never mind," he said abruptly. "Excuse me." He started walking down the path toward the shore. He heard a low snort of laughter behind him.

"Take care you don't get bewitched by the moonlight, my friend," the Duque de Alzacar called. "I'd hate to be soon attending one of these events for *you*…"

Sharif ignored him. Holding up a hand to tell his bodyguards to remain behind, in the shadows of the villa, he went down to the thicket of trees. Where was she? Had he lost her?

Had he dreamed her?

He saw a flash of movement and exhaled. She had moved farther down the shore. He followed silently in his white robes, stalking her like one of the lions that had existed in his Makhtari homeland centuries before.

She moved so sensually. He heard her softly whispered voice. Sharif's eyes narrowed to see whom she was speaking with, but there was no one. Half expecting her to disappear, he came out into the clearing beside her, feeling suddenly clumsy as he stepped on a branch.

At the sound, the woman whirled to face him. They stared at each other.

She wasn't dressed in white, as he'd first thought, but in a pale pink dress, the color of spring's first blush. Her skin was creamy and smooth, plump cheeks the colour of faint roses, standing out starkly against her long black hair. She was barely over twenty, he guessed, and of middle height. Her features were too strong to be conventionally beautiful, with her sharp nose, slash of dark eyebrows and the determined set to her chin; but her full mouth was tender, and her eyes were deep brown, big and wistful and wise. And they were full of tears.

Looking directly into her face, Sharif caught his breath.

"Who are you?" she whispered.

Sharif blinked. Then frowned. "You don't know who I am?"

She shook her head. "Should I?"

Now Sharif *knew* the woman had to be from another place or time. Everyone knew the playboy sheikh who'd swathed his way through continents of the world's most glamorous women, the Emir of Makhtar who often spent millions of euros on a single evening out with his entourage, who always had six bodyguards close at hand and who was rumored to have a bedroom in his royal palace made entirely out of diamonds—false—and that he'd once offered to buy Manchester United on a drunken whim—true.

Did she truly not know who he was? Or was it a pretense, a way for her to play hard to get? He shrugged but watched her closely as he said, "I'm a wedding guest."

"Oh." She exhaled. "Me, too."

"Why are you crying?"

"I'm not."

He watched as a single tear escaped her lashes to trail down her cheek in the moonlight. "No?"

She wiped her cheek fiercely. "No."

He tilted his head, frowning. "Are you in love with the bridegroom? Is that why you're crying?"

"No!"

"Many women were. Half of the women of London, it is said, wept when they heard Cesare Falconeri was to wed his housekeeper…"

"I'm Emma's friend!"

He tilted his head. "So you're crying because you're planning to betray her, and seduce him after the honeymoon is done?"

She stared at him as if he was crazy. "What kind of women do you hang out with? I would never—I could never—" She shook her head, and wiped her eyes again. "I'm happy for them! They're meant for each other!"

"Ah," Sharif said, bored by such trite, polite

statements. "So it is not him. You weep over some other man."

She grit her teeth. "No…"

"Then what is it?"

"What it is—is none of your business!"

Sharif stepped toward her, just two of them hidden behind a copse of trees on the shore of the lake. They were almost close enough to touch. He heard her intake of breath as she took an involuntary step back. Good. So she was aware of him then, as he was of her, no matter her feisty words.

Her eyes held infinite depths, he thought, like a night filled with stars and shadows. He felt strangely dazzled. He'd never seen eyes so full of warmth and buried secrets. Secrets he wanted to learn. Warmth he wanted to feel against his skin.

It was also possible he was just desperate to be distracted from his own thoughts. If so, this woman offered a very pleasurable distraction indeed.

Lifting his eyebrow, Sharif gave her the smile no woman could resist—at least, none ever had—deliberately unleashing the full power of his attention on her. "Tell me why you're crying, *signorina*," he said softly. "Tell me why you left the wedding party and came down to the shore alone."

Her lips parted, then closed. She looked away. "I told you. I'm not crying."

"Just as you also told me you have no idea who I am."

"Correct."

If she was lying about the one, Sharif decided, she was likely lying about the other. Good to know where he stood. He slowly looked up and down her body. The pale pink dress fit her like a glove. She was so curvaceous. So...different.

She blushed beneath his gaze, becoming more impossibly desirable than ever. Sharif suddenly realized it wasn't just his desire to forgot about weddings and marriage that made him want her. He'd been bored for a long, long time. He craved different. He craved this woman.

And so, he would have her.

Why not?

Whether she knew who he was or not, whether she was truly ignorant of his identity or merely putting on an act in an attempt to gain his attention, this woman was nothing truly magical or rare, no matter what his body was telling him. She was different from his usual type, yes. But beyond that, she was nothing more than a beautiful stranger. And he knew exactly how to deal with a beautiful stranger.

"The night is growing cold." Sharif's voice was a low purr as he held out his arm. "Come back to the villa. We will continue this conversation over champagne. Over dinner."

"W-with you?" she stammered, looking startled. She didn't move.

He cast a quick glance to her left hand. "You are not married. Are you engaged?"

She shook her head.

"I didn't think so," he said.

She lifted her head sharply. "You can tell?"

He bared his teeth in a sensual smile. "You are just not the married type."

To his surprise, she looked furious. More than furious. She looked as if he'd just served her a mortal insult.

"And why is that?" she said coldly.

Because of what he was planning to do to her tonight. Because of the delectable images that had started forming in his mind from the instant he'd seen her, of her curvaceous body naked against his, as her plump lips softly moaned against his skin. It had been impossible—absolutely impossible—that fate would be so cruel to have her already bound to another.

But Sharif didn't think it strategically advisable to explain. Not when her dark eyes were glinting sparks of rage.

He frowned, observing the flush on her cheeks. "Why are you angry? What could I possibly have said to—ah." His eyes crinkled in sudden understanding. "I see."

"See what?"

"The reason you came down to the shore, in this quiet, hidden place." He lifted a dark eyebrow knowingly. "I forget how women are affected by weddings. You no doubt wept through the candlelit ceremony, in romantic dreams at the beauty of *love*." His lip curled at the word. "There is some boy back home that you wish would propose. You feel alone. That is why you were crying. That is why you are angry. You are tired of waiting for your lover."

She pulled back, looking as if she'd been slapped.

"You are so wrong," she choked out. "About everything."

"I am pleased to hear it," Sharif murmured, and he was. If there was no other man in the picture, his path to her bed would be a foregone conclusion. "In that case…whatever your reason for sadness, there will be no more tears tonight. Only enjoyment and pleasure. You are spending the evening with me." His eyes met hers. "Not just the evening, but the night."

He continued to hold out his arm in complete assurance. But the woman just stared at him. Her lips parted as she said faintly, "That's your idea of small talk?"

He gave her a sensual smile. "I believe in cutting through unnecessary words to get to the heart of things."

"Then you believe in being rude." Still not touching him, she lifted her chin. "Excuse me."

And without another word, she walked around him, as if the billionaire Emir of Makhtar were no better than a churlish boy. She walked fleet-footed up the path, heading toward the eighteenth-century villa on the hillside, where music and laughter wafted through the cool November night.

Twisting his head, Sharif stared up after her in shock.

Waiting for your lover.
Waiting for your lover.

The rhythm of the darkly handsome sheikh's words seemed to taunt Irene Taylor's footsteps as she went back up the path.

Waiting for your lover.

Irene blinked back tears. With unthinking cruelty he'd spoken the exact fear that had haunted her heart throughout her friend's beautiful wedding. The words that had driven her to leave the other guests to stand alone on the lakeshore in quiet, silent heartbreak. She was twenty-three years old, and she'd been waiting for her lover all her life. She was starting to think he wasn't coming.

She'd dreamed of the life she wanted, the home she wanted, since she was five years old and she'd come home crying from her first day of kindergarten. Her own house was silent, but their closest neighbor had seen Irene walk by, crying and snuffling with a broken lunch box in her hand. Dorothy Abbott had taken her in, wiped the blood off her forehead, given her a big homemade cookie and a glass of milk. Irene had been comforted—and dazzled. How wonderful it would be to live in a little cottage with a white picket fence, baking cookies, tending a garden, with an honest, loyal, loving man as her husband. Ever since that day, Irene had wanted what Dorothy and Bill Abbott had had, married for fifty-four years, caring for each other until the day they'd died, one day apart.

Irene had also known what she *didn't* want. A rickety house on the desolate edge of a small town. Her mother, drunk most of the time, and her much older sister, entertaining "gentlemen" at all hours, believing their lying words, taking their money afterward. Irene had vowed her life would be different, but still, after high school, she'd worked at minimum-wage jobs, trying to save money for college, falling short when her mother and sister inevitably needed her meager earnings.

When Dorothy and Bill died, she'd felt so alone and sad that when the mayor's son smiled at her, she'd fallen for him. Hard. Even when she should have known better.

Funny how it was Carter who'd finally managed to drive her out of town.

I just wanted to have some fun with you, Irene.

That's all. You're not the type I'd marry. He'd given an incredulous laugh. *Did you actually think a man like me, with my background...and a woman like you, with yours...could ever...?*

Yes, she had. She wiped her nose, which was starting to snuffle. Thank heaven she hadn't slept with Carter two years ago. Just the humiliation of loving him had been enough to make her flee Colorado, first for a job in New York, then Paris.

She'd told herself she wanted a fresh start, in a place no one knew about her family's sordid history. But some secret part of her had dreamed, if she went away, she might return self-assured and stylish and thin, like in an Audrey Hepburn movie. She'd dreamed she'd return to her small Colorado town in a sleek little suit with a sophisticated red smile, and Carter would take one look at the New Her and want to give her his love. Not just his love, but his name.

Stupid. It made Irene's cheeks burn to think about it now. She wiped the tears away fiercely. As if living in New York or Paris, as if mere *geography*, could achieve such a miracle—turning *her* into the type of woman Carter would want to marry! As if designer clothes and a new hairstyle would make him take her away from the shabby house on the wrong side of the tracks, the one that had men sneaking in so often at night on paid "dates" with her mother and older sister, to the enormous hundred-year-old Linsey Mansion on the hill!

Well, she'd never know now. Instead, she'd be going home even worse off than she'd left—unemployed, broke and with all the baguettes and croissants she'd eaten in Paris, not exactly thinner, either.

She'd thought she could make a better life for herself. Even after the unfortunate incident that had gotten her fired six months ago, she'd still held out hope she'd find a new job in Paris. She'd gone through her savings, even the precious thousand-dollar bequest that the Abbotts had left her when they died.

Irene stopped. She pressed her fingers against her eyes, trying not to feel the jagged pain in her throat.

There will be no more tears tonight. Only enjoyment and pleasure. She could still hear his low, husky voice. *You are spending the evening with me. Not just the evening, but the night.*

Why her?

She'd always tried to believe it was just her family's reputation that made people in her home town so cruel. That it wasn't personal. But if that was true, why had the dark sheikh immediately assumed the worst of her, asking if she intended to seduce Emma's husband—as if she would want to! As if she could! Why had he assumed she would immediately fall into bed with him, just for the asking?

Irene closed her eyes, brushing her forehead with a trembling hand. Her cheeks were hot. All right, so she'd been attracted to him. How could any woman not be?

How could any woman not be attracted to a man like that, dressed so exotically in full white robes, with his black eyes and cruel, sensual lips? Anyone would be attracted to that darkly handsome face. To his strong, broad-shouldered body. To the aura of power and limitless wealth that followed him like his entourage of bodyguards.

If Carter was out of her league, then this sheikh was so far out of her league that she couldn't even see his league. It was somewhere out in space. Possibly by Jupiter.

Why would a man like that be interested in her?

It was true that for Emma's sake, Irene had done her best to look nice today, brushing out her black hair, putting on makeup. She'd even worn contact lenses instead of her usual soda-bottle glasses, and had on a beautiful, borrowed designer dress. But that didn't explain it.

Had she just seemed like easy pickings, crying by the lake? Or was there something wrong with her, some black mark on her soul that only men like Carter and the sheikh could see?

She remembered how the man's piercing black

eyes had looked right through her soul, seeing far too much.

You feel alone. That is why you were crying. That is why you are angry. You are tired of waiting for your lover.

Pushing the memory of his low, sardonic voice away, she took a deep breath.

She couldn't go back to Colorado. She *couldn't.* But all she had left was twenty euros, a studio apartment in Paris paid for till the end of the week and the return flight home.

Hearing the clanging of a bell, Irene looked up the hill to the highest terrace. Beneath the wisteria-covered trellis with hanging fairy lights, she saw Emma, now Mrs. Falconeri, summoning her guests to the outdoor dinner reception. Emma's new husband, Cesare Falconeri, smiled down at his new bride as their baby son, dressed in a tiny tuxedo, yawned in his arms.

Emma had found her true love, married him, had a baby with him. They were blissfully happy. And kind-hearted. Also, Cesare was a billionaire hotel tycoon, which couldn't hurt anything. Without asking her, they'd simply tucked a first-class airline ticket from Paris to Lake Como in their wedding invitation. *First-class.* She smiled wistfully. Now, *that* had been an experience. The flight attendant had waited on her hand and foot, as if she were someone important. Crazy.

The truth was, she didn't need first-class. She just needed to believe that someday she might have what Emma had, and what Dorothy Abbott had once had: a husband she could love, respect and trust. A happy, respectable life, raising children in a snug, warm home.

She slowly walked up the hill with the other guests. The shadowy terrace was long, filled with three large communal tables placed end to end down the middle, decked out with flowers and glowing candles and colored lights dangling from above. Irene shivered in the November air, in spite of four heat lamps at the corners of the terrace, all going full blast.

She looked at the happy couple holding their fat, adorable baby, trying to ignore how her heart was aching. She was happy for Emma, she truly was. But she wondered at times if she would ever have the same.

Swallowing hard, Irene turned away. And walked right into a hard wall of muscle.

She gasped, her high-heeled shoes sliding beneath her. She started to fall to the stone floor, but a strong hand reached out to grab her wrist.

"Thank you…" Then she saw the face of the wall that had caught her: the handsome, arrogant sheikh, in the white robes with that darkly handsome face and piercing eyes.

"Oh," she scowled. "It's you."

He said nothing in reply, just lifted her to her feet. She felt the warmth and heat of his palm against her skin. It did strange things to her. He looked down at her in the moonlight on the villa's veranda as wedding guests laughed and ambled beneath the fairy lights dangling from the trellis beneath the deep violet Italian sky.

She ripped her arm away. *"Thank you,"* she repeated, in a hostile tone directly at odds with the courtesy of the words.

But he did not immediately turn and leave as she'd hoped. Instead, he stared down at her, his eyes as black as the cord wrapped around his white headdress.

"You accused me of being rude, *signorina*," he said in a low voice. "I was not."

Unconsciously, Irene rubbed her wrist, as if he had burned it with his touch. "You insulted me."

"When I invited you to spend the night with me?" He sounded almost bewildered. "How was that an insult?"

"Are you kidding? What else could it be?"

He looked bemused. "Women generally take it as a compliment…"

Irene flinched. *Women.* Of course he'd used the line a million times, on a million interchangeable women!

"How lovely for you," she said coldly, "that ten

words can usually make any woman fall into bed with you. Sorry I'm not following your agenda."

His lips had parted slightly. His brow was furrowed as he stared down at her. "Have we met before?" he said faintly. "Do you have some reason to despise me?"

"We've never met before, if that's what you're asking. But yes," she said grimly, "I have a reason."

"Which is?"

"Look, I have no idea who you are or why you decided to make me your target, but I know your type."

"My—type?"

"Do you really want me to spell it out? It might hurt your feelings. But then—" she tilted her head "—fortunately I don't think you have any."

"Try me," he said flatly.

"I could say that you're a heartless playboy who accused me, within five seconds of meeting me, of planning to seduce my friend's new husband. Saying I was waiting for a lover and oh, lucky me, you're the very man for the job! How dare you pretend you can see into my soul, and poke at my heart in a rude and selfish way? Those are the things I could say, but I won't, because it's Emma's wedding and she deserves a perfect day. I don't want to cause a scene. Because I was taught that if you can't say something nice to someone, to say nothing at all." Dorothy Abbott had taught her that over oatmeal cookies and peppermint tea. She glared at him. "Some people," she said sweetly, "have good manners. If you'll excuse me."

She started to turn, but he held on to her wrist. She glared at his hand, then at his face. He abruptly let her go.

"Of course, *signorina*," the handsome sheikh said, holding up both his hands. "You are right. I was rude. Please allow me to apologize." His lips twisted. "The better I know you, the more I realize the great mistake I made. Of course you do not want a lover. No sane man would ever want to be *your* lover. It would be like seducing a cactus." He gave her a short half bow with a sweep of his robes. "Please forgive me, *signorina*. And do not allow me to keep you from your eternally desirable solitude."

In a single smooth movement, he turned away from her. Irene stared after him, open-mouthed, as he disappeared into the crowd.

She closed her mouth with a snap.

Ooh! Helplessly, she stomped her foot. *Eternally desirable solitude!* The big jerk!

But at least now he was no longer looking at her—near her—touching her, it was easier to think straight. She was relieved to no longer be under the intense scrutiny of his black eyes, his gaze that seemed to see straight through her soul.

She'd wanted to get rid of him, and she'd succeeded. She did know his type. Well—not *exactly*. A wealthy sheikh in full robes, with bodyguards hovering, was rare in Colorado. Even her mother and older sister had never managed to bring home someone *that* exotic. But she knew the playboy type. She hadn't judged him unfairly. She *hadn't*.

But still—she thought of those dark eyes. Of the way her heart had pounded in the moonlight when she'd first seen him standing in front of her on the lake, the very instant after she'd wished with such reckless, passionate yearning that someone would love her. Of the sizzle that had coursed through her body when he'd touched her—just from the touch of his hand on her wrist!

It was good she'd managed to scare him off. *No sane man would ever want to be* your *lover.* Yup. She'd scared him off thoroughly.

Good, she told herself. Better to be alone, better to be a virgin forever, than have her heart trampled into nothing.

She wanted more.

After her first day of kindergarten, when Dorothy had comforted her and Bill had gone to the school to set the bullies straight, Irene had started spending her afternoons with the retired couple. She'd tried to pretend the Abbotts' tiny, warm house was her real home. When she was older, trying to ignore the cruel taunts of the girls and blatant come-ons of the boys in high school, Irene had once asked Dorothy how she and Bill had found each other. Dorothy had smiled.

"We got married at eighteen, both virgins, nervous and broke. Everyone thought we were too young." She'd laughed, and taken another sip of peppermint tea. "But we knew what we wanted. Waiting made it special, a commitment between us. I know these days, people think sex is no big deal, a moment of cheap pleasure, easily forgotten. But to us, it was sacred. A promise without words. And we never regretted the choice."

Hearing the story when she was eighteen herself, Irene had vowed to wait for true love, too. She'd watched her sister and mother have so many cheap, forgettable affairs until there was no promise left in it, very little pleasure and certainly no joy. She wanted a different life. Her love would last.

She'd nearly gone astray with Carter, but never again. No way. No how. And if there was one thing she knew down to her bones, it was that a man like the sheikh—exotically handsome and rich and full of himself—would never truly love her, not even for an hour, much less a lifetime. She'd been right to scare him off.

But still, as Irene looked for her assigned place at the long wooden table, she was relieved to see it was on the opposite end from the sheikh's place.

As the twenty or so wedding guests had a hearty dinner on the terrace, surrounded by heat lamps to make the November night feel like summer, he kept his distance. Irene tried not to look in his direction, but she felt his dark eyes on her. Taking her heart in her hands, she dared to look down the long table—only to discover that he was laughing, as two gorgeous young supermodel types fawned over him. Irene looked away grumpily. Silly her, to imagine he'd been staring at her. She couldn't imagine why on earth she'd thought that....

The fairy lights hung above, swaying in the breeze. The moon was bright like a big pearl in the velvety sky. After the champagne toast and the delicious dinner served by the villa's staff, the long tables were pushed aside to turn the veranda into an impromptu dance floor. A dark-haired man with soulful eyes brought a guitar from the music room and started to play.

She saw a flash of white in the corner of her eye, and her body went on high alert. But, turning, she saw it was only Emma, holding out her baby. "Will you hold him so we can have our first dance?"

"I'd love to," Irene said, smiling, happy to cuddle the warm, sleeping baby. But after she had Sam in her arms, she had a sudden thought and touched Emma's arm. "There's a sheikh here— one of your guests. Who is he?"

Emma blinked, then frowned in a very "*un-*

happiest day of my life" kind of way. Looking to the right and left, she lowered her head until her white translucent veil dripped to the floor. "*That* is Sheikh Sharif al-Aktoum, the Emir of Makhtar."

"Emir?" Irene said, amazed. "You mean, the king? Of a whole country?"

"Yes." Straightening, Emma gave her a hard stare full of meaning. "He's very rich, very powerful and *very* famous for breaking many, many, *many* women's hearts."

"I was just curious."

"Don't be too curious about him." She shook her head and said severely, "Just because Cesare reformed from being a playboy, you mustn't expect that any other man…"

"I forgot about that," Irene said. "Cesare used to be a playboy, too…"

Emma sighed. "He was. It used to be my job to buy designer watches as parting gifts for his one-night stands. I actually bought them in bulk. But the point is, Irene, most playboys never change. You know that, don't you?"

Her friend looked so anxious that Irene gave her a reassuring nod. "Definitely."

"Good."

As Irene sat back into her chair with the baby, the new Mr. and Mrs. Falconeri went out alone on the dance floor, hand in hand. Swaying to the music, they looked at each other tenderly and passionately, as if no one else were there. Watching them, wistfulness filled Irene's heart.

Someday...

Someday, a man would look at her like that. And she'd have a baby like this. She looked at the warm, slumbering little boy in her arms, with his dark lashes fluttering against his plump cheeks. When the time was right, when fate meant it to be so, she would meet the One. They'd fall in love and get married. They'd work hard, buy a home, have children of their own. They would do things properly.

But what if it never happened? What if she spent her whole life waiting, working hard, following all the rules, and still ended up broke and alone?

Believe. She squeezed her eyes shut. *Have faith.*

"You are not dancing, *fräulein?*"

She looked up with an intake of breath, but instead of the Emir of Makhtar, she saw a dignified blond man with blue eyes. She shook her head, feeling awkward. "No, thank you." Then, remembering how the sheikh had so *unfairly* and *wrongly* compared her to a cactus, she forced herself to smile until her cheeks hurt as she indicated the sleeping baby in her arms. "It's kind of you, but I can't, I'm holding Sam while they dance."

"Ah." The man sighed and said with a German accent, "Such a pity."

"Yes. Indeed," she said, relieved beyond all

measure when he moved on. She didn't know how to react. Two men hitting on her in one night? This had never happened during her year in Paris. But then—she looked down at the sleek-fitting designer gown—she didn't usually dress like this, either. But still, she wasn't half as glamorous or beautiful or thin as the other female guests. Not even close!

Irene knew her flaws. Her thick black hair was her one vanity, but other than that… Her body was too plump. Her nose turned up at the end, and her eyesight was truly bad. She blinked hard. Her new contact lenses still felt strange against her eyeballs. She was used to wearing glasses. She was also used to being invisible. She was used to avoiding attention, staying at home reading books, quietly unnoticed in the corner. She thought longingly of the new Susan Mallery novel waiting on her bedside table.

"Good evening, *señorita*."

Irene looked up at the deep, purring voice. It was the Spanish man who'd been playing the guitar so beautifully.

"You're amazing," she blurted out.

The Spaniard gave a wicked grin. "Who told?"

She blushed. "Your music, I mean. But if you're here, then who…" She turned and saw there was now a four-person band playing the music. She hadn't even noticed the change. She finished lamely, "You are very good on the guitar."

"The least of my skills, I assure you. Would you care to dance?"

"Oh." Her blush deepened. Another handsome playboy, way out of her league, flirting with her? Weird. Had Emma slipped a ten-dollar bill to the most handsome guests in an attempt to boost Irene's confidence? Although these didn't seem like the type of men to be swayed by a ten-dollar bill. Ten million dollars, maybe. Maybe not even then.

Biting her lip, she again indicated the sleeping baby. "Sorry. Emma left me in charge. I'd have only stepped on your feet anyway." She added hastily, "Thanks, though!"

"Another time, perhaps," the Spaniard murmured, and moved on without any apparent heartbreak to one of the wealthy-supermodel types she'd seen the sheikh talking to earlier. Irene looked down at the warm, sleeping baby in her lap. At least she didn't need to worry that anyone had paid little Sam to pretend to like her.

"It must be exhausting," a man's sardonic voice observed behind her, "that the ruder you become, the more you have to beat potential lovers off with a stick."

Irene felt a shock of electricity through her body. She turned her head to see the sheikh standing behind her, his black eyes gleaming. She hid the uncontrollable leap of her heart.

"You would know," she murmured, looking at him sideways beneath her lashes. "Isn't that how it usually works for you? You tell women that they mean nothing to you, that they're just the next mark on your bedpost, and they are so enamored of this thought that they fall at your feet and beg you, *Take me, take me now*?"

His dark eyes held a bright gleam as he took another step toward her.

"Say those five words to me, Miss Taylor," he said softly, "and see what happens."

A tremble electrified her body, from her earlobes down her spine to the hollows of her feet. She licked her lips and tossed her head.

"That's one thing I'll never say to you. Not in a million years."

"I could make you say it, I think," he said softly. "If I really tried."

He looked down at her with eyes black and hot as smoldering coals, and her throat went dry. She felt her body turning into putty, her brain into mush.

"Don't bother trying," she managed to croak. "You'll fail."

He tilted his head. "I don't fail."

"Never?"

"No."

As they stared at each other, the air thickened between them. Something sizzled, something primal. The people around them became blurs of color, mere noise. Held in his dark gaze, Irene felt time stand still.

Then her heart started to beat again. "You used my name. How did you know? Did you ask about me?"

He lifted a dark eyebrow. "I was curious."

"I know about you now, too. The famous playboy emir."

He tilted his head toward her, as if confiding a secret. "I know something about you, too, Miss Taylor."

"What's that?"

With a slow, sensual smile, the billionaire emir held out his hand.

"The reason you refused to dance with those other men," he said huskily, "is because you want to dance with me."

CHAPTER TWO

THE INTENSITY AND focus of his gaze held her down like a butterfly with a pin, leaving her helpless and trembling. Irene's heart pounded in her chest.

"I want to dance with you, Miss Taylor." The sheikh looked down at her. "I want it very much."

Her throat was dry, her mind scrambling. She exhaled when she remembered Sam sleeping in her arms. "Sorry, but I couldn't possibly. I promised to hold the baby and…"

Unfortunately at that moment Sam's mother brushed past them to scoop her sleeping baby up in her arms. "It's time to put this sleepy boy to bed," Emma said, holding him snug against her beaded white gown. She threw the sheikh a troubled glance and said in a low voice to Irene, "Be careful."

"You don't need to worry," Irene said. Really, couldn't her friend see that she could look out for herself? She wasn't *totally* naive.

"Good," Emma murmured, then turned and said brightly to the sheikh, "Excuse me."

Irene looked at him, wondering how much of the whispered conversation he'd heard. One glance told her he'd heard everything. He gave her an amused smile, then lifted a dark eyebrow.

"It's just a dance," he drawled. He tilted his head. "Surely you're not afraid of me."

"Not even slightly," she lied.

"In that case..." Holding out his hand with the courtly formality of an eighteenth-century prince waiting for his lady, he waited.

Irene stared at his outstretched hand. She hesitated, remembering how her body had reacted the last time they'd touched, the way he'd made her tremble with just a touch on her wrist. But as he'd said, this time he was just asking for a dance, not a hot, torrid affair. They were surrounded by chaperones here.

One dance, and she'd show them both that she wasn't afraid. She could control her body's response to him. One dance, and he'd stop being so intrigued by her refusals and leave her safely alone for the rest of the weekend. He'd move on to some other, more responsive woman.

Slowly, Irene placed her hand in his. She gave an involuntary shudder when she felt the electricity as their fingers intertwined, and she felt the heat of his skin pressing against her own.

His handsome face was inscrutable as he led her out onto the terrace's impromptu dance floor. Above them, dappled moonlight turned wisteria vines into braided threads of silver, like magic.

He held her against his body, leading her, swaying her against him as they moved to the music. He looked at her, and Irene felt her body break out in a sweat even as a cool breeze trailed off the moonlit lake against her overheated skin.

"So, Miss Taylor," he murmured, "tell me the real reason you were pushing me away—along with every other man here."

She swallowed, then looked at him. "I will tell you. If you tell me something first."

"Yes?"

"Why you have continued to pursue me anyway." She looked at the women watching them enviously from the edge of the dance floor. "Those other women are far more beautiful than I. They clearly want to be in your arms. Why ask me to dance, instead of them? Especially when it seemed likely I would say no?"

He swirled her around to the music, then stopped. "I knew you wouldn't say no."

"How?"

"I told you. I never fail to get what I want. I wanted to dance with you. And I knew you wanted the same."

"So arrogant," she breathed.

"It's not arrogant if it's true."

Irene's heart was pounding. "I only agreed to dance with you so you'd see that there's nothing special about me, and leave me in peace."

His lips lifted at the corners. "If that was your intention, then I am afraid you have failed."

"I'm boring," she whispered. "Invisible and dull."

His hands brushed against her back as they danced.

"You're wrong. You are the most intriguing woman here. From the moment I saw you on the edge of the lake, I felt drawn to your strange combination of experience—and innocence." Leaning down, he bent his lips to her ear. She felt the roughness of his cheek brush against hers, inhaled the musky scent of his cologne, felt the warmth of his breath against her skin. "I want to discover all your secrets, Miss Taylor."

He pulled back. She stared up at him, her eyes wide. She tried to speak, found she couldn't. His dark eyes crinkled in smug masculine amusement.

He twirled her to the music, and when she was again in his arms, he said, "I answered your question. Now answer mine. Why have you been pushing every man away who talks to you at this wedding? Do you have something against them personally, or just dislike billionaires on principle?"

"Billionaires?"

"The German automobile tycoon has been married three times, but still considered very eligible by all the gold diggers in Europe. Then, of course, my Spanish friend, the Duque de Alzacar, the second-richest man in Spain."

"Duke? Are you kidding? I thought he was a musician!"

"Would it have changed your answer to him if you'd known?"

"No. I'm just surprised. He's a good guitar player. Rich men usually don't try so hard. They expect other people to entertain *them*. They don't care who else gets their heart bruised trying to win their attention, their love—"

She broke off her words, but it was too late. Aghast, Irene met his darkly knowing glance.

"Go on," he purred. "Tell me more about what rich men do."

She looked away. "You're just not my sort, that's all," she muttered. "None of you."

The sheikh looked around the beautiful moonlit terrace. His voice was incredulous. "A German billionaire, a Spanish duke, a Makhtari emir? We are none of us your type?"

"No."

He gave a low, disbelieving laugh. "You must have a very specific type. The three of us are so different."

She shook her head. "You're exactly the same."

His eyes narrowed. "What do you mean?"

"Your eminence... I'm sorry, what am I supposed to call you?"

"Normally the term 'Your Highness' is the correct form. But since I suspect you are about to insult me, please call me Sharif."

She snorted a laugh. "Sharif."

"And I will call you Irene."

It was musical the way he said it, with his husky low voice and slight inflection of an accent. She had never heard her name pronounced quite that way before. He made it sound—*sensual.* Controlling a shiver, she took a deep breath. As he moved her across the stone floor, they were surrounded by eight other couples dancing. The bride and groom were no longer to be seen, the wine was flowing and the lights in the wisteria above them sparkled in the dark night, swaying in the soft breeze off the lake.

"Explain," he said darkly, "how I am exactly like every other man."

She got the feeling he wasn't used to being compared to anyone, even tycoons or dukes. "Not *every* man. Just, well—" she looked around them "—just all the men here."

Sharif set his jaw, looking annoyed. "Because I asked you to dance?"

"No—well, yes. The thing is," she said awkwardly, "you're all arrogant playboys. You expect women to fall instantly into bed with you. And you're full of yourselves because you're usually right."

"So I am conceited."

"It's not your fault. Well, not *entirely* your fault," she amended, since she wanted to be truthful. "You're just selfish and coldhearted about getting what you want. But when you throw out these lines, these false promises of love, women are naive enough to fall for them."

"*False promises*. So now I am a liar, as well as conceited."

"I am trying to say this gently. But you did ask me."

"Yes. I did." He pulled her closer against his body. She felt his warmth and strength beneath his white robes, saw the black intensity of his gaze. "We were introduced five minutes ago, but you think you know me."

"Annoying, isn't it? Just like you did with me."

Sharif stopped on the dance floor, looking at her. "I have never given any woman a false promise of love. Never."

Irene suddenly felt how much taller he was, how broad-shouldered and powerful. He towered over her in every way, and he had a dangerous glint to his eye that might have frightened a lesser woman. But not her. "Perhaps you haven't actually spoken the promise in words, but I bet you *insinuate*. With your attention. With your gaze. With your touch. You're doing it now."

His hands tightened on her as he pulled her snugly against his body. His hot, dark eyes searched hers as he said huskily, "And what do I insinuate?"

She lifted her troubled gaze.

"That you could love me," she whispered. "Not just tonight, but forever."

For an instant, neither of them moved.

Then she moved her body two inches away from him, a safe distance any high school chaperone would approve of, with their arms barely touching.

"That's why I wouldn't dance with the others," she said. "Why I'm not interested in you or any man like you. Because I know all your sexy charm—it's just a lie."

Sharif stared at her. Then his eyebrow lifted as he gave her a sudden wicked smile.

"So you think I'm sexy and charming."

She looked up at him. "You know I do."

Their eyes locked. Desire shot in waves down her body, filling her with heat. Making her tremble. She felt the electricity between them, felt the warmth and power of his body. Her knees were weak.

Most playboys never change. You know that, don't you?

She hadn't needed Emma's warning. She'd

learned it well. From the wretched lessons of her childhood. From Carter. She'd learned it up close and personal.

She abruptly let Sharif go.

"But you're wasting your time with me." She glanced back at the beautiful women watching him with longing eyes, as if they could hardly wait to throw themselves body and soul onto the fire. Irene's lip curled as she nodded in their direction. "Go try your luck with one of them."

Turning on her heel, she left without a backward glance. Praying he wouldn't see how her body shook as she walked away.

He'd underestimated her.

Sharif's jaw was tight as he stalked off the dance floor alone. He walked through the crowd of watching women, some of whom tried to talk to him as he passed.

"Your Highness, what a surprise…"

"Hello, we met once at a party, if you remember…"

"I'd be happy to dance with you, Your Highness, even if she won't…"

Grimly, he kept walking, without bothering to reply. Perhaps he was rude, after all, just as Irene had accused. But these skinny women, with their glossy red lips and hollow cheekbones, were suddenly invisible to him. It wasn't their fault. All other women were invisible to him now because he was interested in only one.

The one who wasn't afraid to tell him the truth. Who wasn't afraid to insult him. And who found it so easy to walk away.

Miss Irene Taylor. Of Colorado, the wild, mountainous center of the United States he knew only from skiing once in Aspen.

There's nothing special about me.

He shook his head incredulously. How could she honestly believe that?

He wanted her.

He would have her.

But how?

"Having a good time?"

Sharif stopped. It took him a moment to focus on Cesare Falconeri, the bridegroom, standing in front of him in a tux. "Your wedding has been most exciting," he replied. "In fact, the most interesting I've ever attended."

"*Grazie.* Emma will be pleased to hear it." The man gave him a sudden grin. "And this is just the start. Tomorrow, we have the civil ceremony in town, followed by all kinds of fun for the rest of the day, including the ball at night." He clapped him heartily on the shoulder. "So save some energy, Your Highness."

The rest of the weekend. As Cesare walked away, Sharif relaxed, took a deep breath. He still had two days. He felt rebounding confidence. Yes. What was he worried about? He had the rest of the weekend to seduce her. She'd already given so much of her true emotion away—too much. He knew she wanted him. She was fighting her own desire. That never worked for long. Willpower always gave out eventually.

Sharif would win. As long as he had the stamina for a long, drawn-out siege. He thought of her.

He definitely had the stamina.

But how to go about it?

All day tomorrow. A ball lasting far into the night. By the end of it, she would be in his bed. Simple as that.

He would seduce her, bed her, satiate himself with her, and they would part on mutually respectful terms the following morning, after the final breakfast. He dismissed Irene's concern about his playboy nature out of hand. Perhaps she'd be right to fear some kind of emotional fallout if they had some kind of continuing connection. But they did not move in the same circles, so it was highly unlikely. This Italian villa—he looked up at the Falconeri mansion—was a weekend party out of place and time. It would be a pleasant memory for both of them, nothing more. One night together would hardly be enough to inspire love, even in a woman as romantic as Irene Taylor. She might be young, but she had an old soul. He'd seen it in her eyes. Heard it in the tremble of her voice as she spoke about the selfishness of playboys. One must have hurt her, once.

Sharif would distract her from the pain of that memory, as she would distract him from his own pain that lay ahead. He would fill her with pleasure. It would be a night they'd never forget.

She'd won the battle tonight, but he would win the war.

Sharif felt oddly exhilarated as he returned to the villa. One by one, his six bodyguards fell wordlessly into step behind him, then peeled off to their assigned rooms as he returned to his suite, two of them standing guard in the hallway outside his door.

Alone in the lavish bedroom, he smiled to himself as he removed his white *keffiyeh* and black rope of the *agal*. He ran his hands through his short dark hair. His head felt sweaty—and no wonder, since every inch of his body had felt overheated since he'd met the delectable Miss Taylor. He started toward the en suite bathroom for a shower, when he heard the ring of his cell phone.

He glanced at who was calling, and his jaw went tense with irritation. He had no choice but to answer.

"Has something happened with Aziza?" he demanded by way of greeting.

"Well…" Gilly Lanvin, the twentysomething

socialite he'd hired as his young sister's companion, drew out the word as long as she could, clearly scrambling to think of a way to keep him on the phone.

"Is she hurt?" he said tersely. "Does she need me?"

"Nooo…" the woman admitted with clear reluctance. "I was just wondering…when you'll be back to the palace."

"Miss Lanvin," he snapped. "These calls have to stop. You are companion to my sister. Nothing more. It would be inconvenient for me to replace you so soon before her wedding. Do not make me do so."

"Oh, no, Your Highness. I'm sorry if I interrupted you. I just thought you might be lonely. I just thought—"

He clicked off the phone before he was forced to endure hearing what she'd thought. He needed to replace her. He'd known it since she'd first started making eyes at him two months ago. But Aziza liked her. So he'd hoped to just ignore it until Aziza's wedding, when a companion would no longer be required and he could send the woman back to Beverly Hills on the next flight.

Three months. Just three months and his sister would be married, and it would no longer be his problem. He stalked into the gleaming white marble bathroom and removed the rest of his clothes, then stepped into a steaming hot shower. He turned his mind back to the delicious Miss Taylor. He let his imagination run wild, picturing her in this shower with him, naked, as he soaped up those full lush curves of her body, hearing her gasp as he pressed her against the shower wall and took her deep and hard, as her wide-spread hands pressed against the steamed glass...

Oh, yes. Tomorrow night. Sooner, if he was at the top of his skill.

Climbing naked into his large bed, he slept very well that night, dreaming of everything he intended to do to Irene Taylor, in this very suite, before the next day was through.

He woke to see the sun shining gold through the tall windows. Yawning, he stretched in the huge bed, feeling the Egyptian-cotton sheets beneath his skin. Smiling to himself, he brushed his teeth, shaved, dressed with care. Not the traditional Makhtari dress today. Instead, he reached into the closet for a crisp white shirt and suit tailored for him in London. Unlike many men of his position, he preferred having no valet, something that had caused a minor scandal in his palace. But there were some things a man just liked to do for himself. He ran his hands impatiently through his black hair and smiled at himself in the mirror.

He would have her tonight.

Sharif went downstairs to join the other guests

in the breakfast room. Soon, they were joined by the blushing bride and groom, who looked very happy and not a little tired. But there was no sign of Irene. He waited. Even when the other guests piled into the arranged limos, to take them all into town for the civil ceremony, he waited, waving off Falconeri.

"I'm not quite done with my coffee," he'd said by way of explanation. The man gave him a strange look, as if he thought it wasn't an entirely satisfying reason for a guest to miss a wedding. But they all left.

The villa became quiet, except for the low hum of servants preparing the next meal, and his own bodyguards conversing quietly on the edges of the cavernous, brightly painted breakfast room. Five minutes later, he heard high heels clicking rapidly across the marble foyer and sighed in anticipation.

He looked up from his Arabic-language newspaper with a ready smile as Irene burst into the doorway.

"Am I too late?" she cried.

"You just missed them," he replied. "They left five minutes ago."

Irene looked even more beautiful than last night, he thought. She was dressed in black pumps and a 1950s-style day dress that accented her hourglass figure—Valentino? Oscar de la Renta?—topped with a soft pink cardigan and pearls. A smudge of deep pink lipstick was her only makeup, accenting the slight bruise of violet beneath her huge dark eyes that suggested a sleepless night. Perhaps she hadn't found the sensual dreams of them making love quite so comforting and pleasant as he had.

"Dang it!" She hung her shoulders. "I can't believe I overslept. On Emma's special day. I am the worst friend ever!"

"She has *three* special days," he said sharply. "Don't be so hard on yourself. It doesn't matter."

"I can't believe I was so careless." She rubbed her eyes with the back of her hand. "I must have turned off my alarm. I was just so tired, I didn't fall asleep until dawn..."

"Oh?" He tilted his head suggestively. "I'm sorry to hear that. Something keep you awake?"

She opened her mouth, then snapped it closed. "Never mind." She reached for the silver coffeepot and a china cup edged with a pattern of twenty-four-carat gold. As she poured the steaming hot coffee, followed by tons of cream and sugar, she glanced at his paper.

"What are you reading?"

"Today's newspaper from my home country."

"Today's? How did you get it?"

"It was delivered to me by plane."

"Can't you get it online?"

"I like paper."

"So you had a whole plane fly all the way here just because you—"

"Yes," he said. "Just because."

"Ridiculous," she grumbled. Sitting on the very edge of the farthest chair, she sipped her coffee, glaring at him over the rim of her cup. "You expecting some kind of war today?"

"War?" Finishing the last of his espresso, Sharif calmly set the cup back in the saucer.

She looked pointedly at the four bodyguards, all now still as statues in the four corners of the room. "You brought your army along for breakfast?"

"I am Emir of Makhtar," he said, as if it explained everything.

She snorted. "Are you afraid you'll be attacked?" She looked at the cheerful yellow walls, the tall windows overlooking Lake Como, the high ceilings with their early-nineteenth-century frescoes. Her lips lifted. "Clearly this could be dangerous."

He shrugged. "Standard procedure."

"Having four hulking babysitters always hovering around sounds like my idea of hell. Although at least it's easy to get rid of your lovers the morning after."

"Are you looking to start a fight with me, Miss Taylor?"

"You said you were going to call me Irene. And yes, I'm looking to start a fight. It's your fault

I overslept. You're the one who kept me up all night."

He hadn't expected her to admit it so easily. "Dreaming of me?"

"Dreaming?" She looked at him as if he was crazy. "It wasn't a dream I heard all night, banging and moaning in the room next door. It was really quite...athletic, the length and stamina of it all. I'm glad you so eagerly took my advice and found another woman more willing to service you."

"Length?" He looked at her with wickedly glinting eyes. He rubbed his jaw. "Stamina?"

Her cheeks flamed a delectable red. "Forget it."

"I'm flattered you immediately assumed it was me."

"Of course it was you," she snapped. "I don't appreciate how you kept me up all night. Now I've missed Emma's civil ceremony because of you. Next time tell your bed partner to keep her opinion of your acrobatics to herself."

"I appreciate the compliment, but it wasn't me."

"Sure," she said scornfully.

Sharif looked at her.

"It. Wasn't. Me."

She stared at him for a long moment, then her expression changed. "Oh." If anything, she seemed to get even more embarrassed. "Sorry." She wiped her eyes fiercely, tried to laugh. "I really seem to be messing everything up today."

"You are really so upset about missing the civil ceremony?"

She blinked back tears. "I don't miss things like this. I don't. I'm the one that people count on. What if she needs me to take care of the baby during the ceremony? What if she's upset because I'm not there? What if…"

"With all those guests around them, she probably didn't even notice your absence."

"I let her down."

"You slept in. It happens."

"Not to me." She rubbed her hand over her eyes. "I'll never forgive myself for this."

"Why?" he asked gently. "Why are you the only one who has to be perfect?"

"Because if I'm not, then…"

"Then?"

"Then I'm no better than…"

"Who?"

Her china cup clattered against the saucer. Snapping her mouth closed, she shook her head. "It doesn't matter. I failed." She looked away. "It's getting to be a habit."

The last thing Sharif wanted was to endure another wedding, especially one in some dreary Italian registry office. But looking at the misery on her beautiful, plump-cheeked face, he rose from the table. Tossing down his napkin, he went to her. "My car is parked in the barn. My driver is here…"

Irene looked up with an intake of breath. "You'd take me?"

"I'm willing to take you anywhere. Anytime." He lifted an eyebrow wickedly. "I thought that was clear."

She blushed but said stubbornly, "Their wedding…"

"Personally, I think attending one wedding is enough. I have no particular need to see it all replayed out, this time in a civil office. But if it truly matters so much to you…"

"It does!"

"Then I will take you. When you're ready." He hid a private smile.

Chugging down the rest of her sweet creamy coffee, she stood up. "I'm ready now." Warmth and gratitude shone in her brown eyes as she clapped her hands happily, like a child. "I take back every awful thing I said about you!"

Impulsively, she threw her arms around him. He felt her against him, right through the fabric of his suit, to his skin, all the way to blood and bone. His body stirred.

Stiffening, Irene pulled back, her eyes wide. He looked down at her.

"Feel free to kiss me," he said lazily, "if you feel you truly must."

Her expression sharpened, and she pushed away. "On second thought, everything I said about you still stands." She looked with self-consciousness to the right and left at the bodyguards. "When can we leave?"

"Now." Lifting his hand in the smallest signal, he caused the four unsmiling bodyguards to fall in behind them, and they left the villa.

"This feels ridiculous," Irene whispered, holding his arm as she walked close to him. "Don't you feel like…like a prisoner getting escorted to your cell?"

At her words, the trapped feeling rose inside him, the one he'd been trying so hard to avoid, for a reason that had nothing to do with the bodyguards. The thing that had trapped him for twenty years, that was soon to lock him down forever, the thing he'd come to this wedding to try to come to terms with.

"I'm accustomed to it," he said tightly.

She shook her head. "I understand that as a powerful man you need bodyguards, but it just seems like it would be impossible to have any private life, any life at all really, when you have such a thick wall between you and the rest of the…"

Her voice trailed off. Sharif smiled at the dumbfounded look on her face as she stared at his black stretch Rolls-Royce, complete with diplomatic flags, inside the large, modern barn. A uniformed driver leaped to attention, opening the door for them. Sharif indicated for her to go first, something that made his bodyguards look at each other behind their aviator sunglasses. Well, let them wonder about the breach in protocol. Sharif didn't care. He climbed in beside her.

Irene's mouth was wide as she looked around the backseat of the limousine in awe. Seeing him, she kept scooting, pressing herself against the far wall.

"Are you so afraid to be near me?"

"Um." She stopped, looking uncertain. "I was making room."

"Room?"

"For all the bodyguards."

His lips curved. "One of them will sit up with the driver. The rest will follow separately."

"Oh." She paused. "But there's plenty of space. This car is ridiculous."

"I'm glad you approve."

"I didn't say *that*." She stretched out her legs in illustration. "You could fit a football team in here. This space is big enough to be used as a house for a family of—five..."

Her voice trailed off as she caught him looking at her bare legs, and realized that her hemline had pulled halfway up her thigh. Exhaling, she quickly sat up straight, yanking down the hem like a prim Victorian lady. He hid his amusement because he knew by the end of the night he would have stroked and kissed every inch she was trying

to hide from him now. And she would have stroked
and kissed every inch of him. Her defenses would
fall and she would succumb to her own desire.
The passion he sensed beneath her facade, once
unleashed, would burn them both to ash. Let her
try to hide from him now all she wanted. It would
just make conquest all the sweeter.

"What are you smiling about?" she said suspiciously.

"Nothing," he said, still smiling. As the limo
moved down the ribbon of road, he turned his
head to look at the beautiful Italian countryside.
Brilliant golden sunlight brushed his face, dappled
with the shadows of clouds passing across the blue
sky. He was aware of every movement Irene made
in the seat beside him, and relished the hot anticipation building inside him. He couldn't remember
the last time he'd wanted any woman so much.

In a few minutes, the limo and following SUV
pulled up in front of an officious-looking Italian
building clinging to the edge of a cliff, tightly between the lake and the main road through town.
Without even waiting for the driver to open her
door, Irene opened it herself and jumped out.
Standing on the sidewalk, she blinked up at the
building, then glanced back doubtfully.

"Are you sure this is the place?" she asked
Sharif.

"It is the address."

Hesitantly, she followed him into the building. The bodyguards hung back in the hall as Sharif and Irene found the small, gray, official-looking room where the ceremony for Falconeri and his housekeeper bride had just begun. Quietly, they took the last seats in the back, behind the rest of the guests, and watched the couple marry in the civil ceremony.

Even Sharif had to admit the bride looked radiant, in a simple cream-colored silk suit and netted hat, holding her cooing baby son in her lap. The groom looked even more joyful, if that were possible. The Falconeris were the only bright light in a rather gray room.

"They look so happy," Irene whispered.

"It's beautiful," he agreed sardonically.

She flashed him a glance. "It's different from the ceremony last night, that's all."

He gave a low laugh. "Last night was about romance. This is about marriage. The legal, binding contract." A hollow feeling rose in his gut. "Trapping them. To each other. Forever."

Irene's eyes lifted in surprise. Then she scowled. Leaning over, she whispered in his ear, "Look, your royalness, I get how you're deeply uninterested in any sort of emotion that doesn't end up in a one-night stand, but seeing as Cesare is your friend—"

"My business acquaintance," he corrected.

"Well, Emma is my friend, and this is her wedding. If you have any rude thoughts about marriage in general or theirs in particular, keep them to yourself."

"I was just agreeing with you," he protested.

She stared at him, then sighed. "Fine," she said, looking disgruntled. "This setting isn't completely romantic."

Sharif looked at her.

"Unlike you, Miss Taylor," he said softly. "You, I think, are the last truly romantic woman of a cold modern age." He tilted his head. "You really believe, don't you? You believe in the fantasy."

She looked away, staring fiercely at the happy couple.

"I have to," she said almost too softly for him to hear. "I couldn't stand it otherwise. And just look at them. Look at what they have…"

Sharif looked at her. He saw the yearning on her face, the wistful, almost agonized hope.

As the bride and groom spoke the final words that would bind them together forever in the eyes of Italian law, Sharif silently reached for Irene's hand and took it gently in his own. This time, he wasn't thinking about seduction. He was trying to offer comfort. To both of them.

And this time, she didn't pull away.

CHAPTER THREE

"Now, this—" Irene sighed, leaning back on the blanket as she felt the warm Italian sun on her face a few hours later "—is lovely."

"Yes," Sharif's low voice said beside her. "Lovely."

Just the sound of his voice made her heart beat faster. Opening her eyes, she looked at him, lounging beside her on the picnic blanket on the hillside. He'd abandoned his jacket on the way back to the villa. She'd intended to return with the rest of the guests, but he'd convinced her otherwise.

"You're not going to make me go back alone, are you?" he'd asked. "And desert me for a bunch of people you don't care about?"

She'd hesitated, and when she saw that Emma had already left the town in a luxury sedan with Just Married written in a sign on the back, she'd found it impossible to say no.

The truth was that she was starting to…like him. It didn't mean anything, she told herself.

After all, it was only natural that she'd find his company slightly more appealing than that of the rest of the wedding guests, none of whom she knew. Why wouldn't she feel more relaxed around Sharif, especially now that he'd traded the formidable native dress of the Emir of Makhtar for a tailored European suit that made him look exactly like every other man?

Well. Maybe not exactly like every man. And maybe *relaxed* was not the precise word to describe her feelings around him.

Irene shivered.

Stretched beside her on the blanket, Sharif emanated sex appeal, looking impossibly handsome in a gray vest and tie and tailored gray trousers. She licked her lips as her eyes dropped to the sleeves of his white shirt, rolled up to reveal the dusting of dark hair over his tanned forearms.

Just seeing that much of his skin made a bead of sweat break between her breasts that had nothing to do with the warm Italian sun.

He lifted a dark eyebrow, and she realized she'd been staring. And cripes, had she just licked her lips?

"It's...warm for November...isn't it?" she said weakly.

His dark gaze looked amused. "Is it?"

"Haven't you noticed?" She sat up abruptly on the blanket. She was relieved to see the rest of the wedding party and guests picnicking in the post-wedding luncheon farther down the hill. Golden sunlight danced across the field of autumn flowers, in the meadow on the Falconeri estate. Picnic lunches had been arranged for all of them by the picnic butler. Honest to God, a picnic butler. Shaking her head at the memory, Irene reached for the big wicker picnic basket. She licked her lips again, trying to act as if she'd been thinking about only food all the while. "You must be hungry. When I'm hungry, I can't think about anything but cream cakes. You're hungry, right?"

"Starving," he said softly, his dark eyes tracing her. "And you're right. When a man is hungry, everything else stops. Until his craving is satisfied."

Irene had the sudden feeling he wasn't talking about food. A tremble went over her body as she looked at him.

He gave her an innocent smile with his full, sensual lips.

No man should have lips like that, Irene thought. It shouldn't be legal. She suddenly wondered what it would feel like to be kissed by those lips.

No! She couldn't let herself be tempted, not even for a moment. Virginity, once lost, was lost forever. She couldn't let herself be lured by desire, not when the cost for that momentary pleasure would be the life—the committed love—that she really wanted!

She forced herself to look down at the basket. She took out Italian sandwiches on fresh crusty bread, antipasto and fresh fruit salad, all of which she put on elegant china plates before handing one to him, along with a fine linen napkin and a fork she suspected was made of pure silver.

"Thank you," he said gravely.

"Don't mention it," she said, looking away. She noticed the four bodyguards at a distance, in strategic locations on the edges of the meadow. "They really follow you everywhere, don't they? I know you're emir and all, but how can you stand it?"

Sharif used a solid-silver fork to take a bite of antipasto off his elegant china plate. "It is part of my position that I accept."

She shook her head. "But the loss of privacy… I'm not sure it's a great trade-off. Wealth, power, fame. But also four babysitters dogging your feet wherever you go."

"Six." The corners of his lips tilted upward. "The other two are keeping an eye on my room at the villa."

Irene stared at him. "Right." Her voice was heavy with irony. "Because you never know when there might be a sudden attack on *Lake Como.*"

"You never know what the world will bring to your door."

"It's obvious, even to me, that six guards is overkill in a place like—"

"My father was shot down in broad daylight, twenty years ago, while vacationing with my mother." He took a bite of pasta salad. "Shot down by an ex-mistress. In a private, gated villa on the French Riviera."

Irene gave an intake of breath, then set down her forkful of fruit salad. She lifted her tremulous gaze. The hard lines of his face held no emotion.

"I'm so sorry," she whispered. "What…happened?"

"His mistress turned the gun on herself. She died at once. My father bled out on the terrace and died ten minutes later. In my mother's arms."

It was all so horrible, Irene felt sick inside. "I'm so sorry," she said again, helplessly. "How old were you?"

"Fifteen." His mouth pressed into a grim line. "At boarding school in America. A teacher pulled me out of class. Two men I'd never met before bowed to me, calling me the emir. I knew something must have happened to my father but it wasn't until I arrived back at the palace that I discovered what it was." Reaching out with an unsteady hand, he poured a bottle of springwater into one of the glasses. He drank it all in one gulp, then looked away. "It was a long time ago."

She felt awful, needling him about bodyguards when his own father had died in a situation every bit as apparently safe as this. "I'm sorry…you… I'm such a…I can't even imagine…"

"Forget about it." Sharif looked at the rest of the wedding party farther down the meadow. "As you said, today is a day for celebration. What's this?" Reaching into the basket, he pulled out a bottle of expensive champagne. "And still chilled." His lips curved as he looked at the label. "Now, *this* is the right way to endure a wedding."

Endure? She wondered at his choice of words. Then, she could hardly blame him for thinking so ill of romance, love or marriage, when his own parents' marriage had ended as it had.

He looked up, his dark gaze daring her to ask him more about it. Her mouth went dry.

"It's a little early for champagne, isn't it?" was all she could manage.

Without answering, Sharif popped the bottle open and poured it into two crystal glasses. He held one out to her, with a smile that didn't meet his eyes.

"Surely you, Miss Taylor, with your romantic nature," he drawled, "would not refuse a glass of champagne to celebrate your dearest friend's happy day?"

When he put it like that… "Well, no." She took the glass. "And for heaven's sake. Call me Irene."

Sharif looked down at her across the blanket.

"Irene," he said in a low voice.

Sensuality and power emanated from him in a way that fascinated her. In a way that was dangerous. Her eyes fell to his lips. To the slight shadow of scruff on his sharp jawline. To his neck.

Forcing herself to look away, she drank deeply from her glass. She'd never tasted champagne before, and it was every bit as delicious and bubbly and intoxicating as it looked in the movies. Sitting here in the meadow, beside a sexy Makhtari emir, overlooking a two-hundred-year-old Italian villa with the blue sparkling lake beyond, Irene felt as if she, too, had been transported into a movie, or a dream.

They ate in silence. With no words to fill the air, she was even more aware of Sharif's every movement. She looked at him sideways through her lashes, at the gleam of golden sunlight against his tawny skin. The thick shape of his throat above his white collar and blue tie. His long, muscled legs beneath the well-tailored trousers. She felt a cool breeze on her own overheated cheeks and the bare legs peeking out from her dress. But just as she was desperately trying to think of something to talk about, he abruptly spoke into the silence.

"So, you live in Paris?"

It was such a small-talk sort of salvo, it surprised her. Irene suddenly wondered if, in spite of Sharif being a powerful, rich sheikh, he might also be a person, who himself might have been trying to think of conversation, just as she had been.

"I had a job there. As a nanny for the Bulgarian ambassador's children."

"Had?"

She ate some fruit salad. "I was, um, fired."

He looked shocked. "You?"

"I loved the children, but…their parents and I had some creative differences." She took a big bite of sandwich and chewed slowly, but after she swallowed, he was still waiting patiently for her to continue. She sighed. "I've never been good at holding my tongue. I felt the parents were spending too much time at parties and entertaining, and were neglecting the emotional needs of their girls and needed to get their priorities straight."

He lifted his eyebrows. "And you—said this—to them?"

"I've always had a problem with telling the truth."

"You mean the problem is that you actually tell it?" He gave a low laugh, and she loved the sound. So sexy. So warm. It made his dark eyes light up in a way that melted her inside.

"Don't laugh," Irene said. "You're a billionaire and a king. I bet no one tells you the truth about anything. They're too scared."

"I doubt that very much." He gave another laugh, but this time there was no warmth in it.

"I wish some of my servants were a little more afraid, to tell you the truth. My sister has a companion who—"

He cut himself off.

"You have a sister?"

"Yes." He looked away.

Birds sang above them, echoing plaintively across the valley. Feeling awkward, Irene lifted her glass to her lips to take a fortifying drink of champagne, only to discover she'd finished it already. How had that happened?

"Allow me." Sharif brought the bottle to her glass. Placing his hand over hers, to steady her hold on the crystal stem, he tilted the bottle against the lip and poured deeply into her glass. Irene felt his larger hand over hers, felt the warmth of his palm against her skin, and a deep shudder went through her.

She looked up at his darkly handsome face.

"So where are you working now?" he asked.

She licked her lips. "I'm, um, not."

"Taking time off?"

"I'm sadly between jobs," she said lightly. "It's been six months. I'm running out of money."

Sharif frowned. "Can't Mrs. Falconeri arrange a job for you at one of her husband's hotels?"

"She probably could, if I asked her. But I won't."

"No desire to work in the hotel business?"

"It's not that. I wouldn't dream of presuming on our friendship that way. It wouldn't be right."

He was staring at her as if she were crazy. "What are you talking about?"

She glared at him. "I'm not that kind of person, okay? Feelings are feelings, friends are friends, and I'm not going to use any relationship for financial gain. I won't. I'm not like—"

Like my family, she almost said, but cut herself off just in time.

Or maybe she didn't. Sharif was looking at her with consternation. As if seeing her for the first time.

"What happened?" he said in a low voice. "I thought some man broke your heart. But it's more than that, isn't it? Or else why wouldn't you ask a good friend for help finding a job? Why would you be afraid?"

"I'm not afraid!" Her cheeks flamed. "I just prefer to find a job on my own, that's all. I don't need Emma's help." She wouldn't let him see into her soul. She wouldn't. "Don't worry about me, Your Highness," she said coldly. "I'll be fine."

He looked as if he didn't believe her. His lips parted, as if he was about to ask her questions she wouldn't want to answer.

Looking down across the meadow, she rose unsteadily to her feet. "Let's pack up. I'm done."

But after they'd silently packed the dishes and

he'd folded the blanket, as she started to walk ahead of him, Sharif caught her arm.

"Wait." Tilting his head, he gave her an impish, sideways smile. "Before we rejoin the other guests, I have something to show you."

An hour later, Irene was still staring at it in shock.

"You've got to be kidding," she said for the sixth time. She tilted her head, regarding it from the other direction. Nope. It still didn't look real. It was too outrageously huge, too ridiculous to be believed.

Beside her, Sharif tilted his head as well, looking down at it with poorly concealed masculine smugness. "Like it?"

Irene licked her lips, trying to find the words.

"A little too big?" he offered finally.

She looked up at him. "You think?"

"It's purely for your pleasure."

"I didn't ask for anything that huge."

"You didn't ask for anything at all. But I knew you wanted it. Every woman does."

Irene bit her lip, staring at it.

"Touch it," he said encouragingly. "Go on. Don't be afraid. It won't bite."

"That's what you think," she muttered, but finally, the temptation was too much to resist. It was too spectacular not to touch. She wanted to feel it for herself, every hard delicious curve.

Reaching out, she gently stroked her fingertips over the diamond necklace he was holding out in the black velvet case.

The diamonds felt hard and smooth. Especially the center five stones, which had to be well over ten carats...each. They sparkled from the fire inside them.

Just as she did when she was near Sharif.

"Put it on," he said, coming closer. "You know you want to."

Yanking back her hand, she shook her head, setting her jaw. "I couldn't possibly accept."

"Why not?"

She looked at him in disbelief. "You really have to ask? After I told you how I feel about mixing the lines between relationships and financial gain?"

Sharif lifted a dark eyebrow.

"Why, Miss Taylor. Are we in a *relationship*?" he purred. "Am I to understand you cannot accept my small gift because you've fallen desperately in love with me?"

He'd caught her very neatly.

"Of course not," she said, glaring at him.

"In that case..."

He pulled her to the full-length mirror in his bedroom suite. Removing her borrowed band of Emma's pearls, he replaced them with the diamond necklace from the black velvet box.

She nearly gasped at the cool weight of the stones against her skin.

"You look beautiful," Sharif said softly, standing behind her. "You will be the queen of the ball tonight."

"No one will be queen but Emma," Irene said. "It's her day." Then she swallowed as she looked at herself in his mirror.

Afternoon sunlight was beaming down from the tall windows of his bedroom. She saw her own big eyes, the pink flush on her cheeks, her full, trembling lips. In her borrowed Lela Rose dress, with the diamonds flashing fire against her skin, she did look like a queen. But she couldn't kid herself it was the dress, or even the jewels that made her look so...alive.

It was the man standing behind her now. She couldn't touch him. But she could touch this...

Unthinkingly, she raised her hand and ran it down the thick, hard jewels. "How much did it cost?"

"It's not good manners to ask, is it?"

"How much?" she demanded.

He shrugged. "A minor amount that I can easily afford."

Irene licked her lips, still staring at herself in the mirror. *Take it off this instant*, she ordered herself, but she found her hand wouldn't obey. Instead of reaching back to undo the clasp at her nape, it was stroking the huge jewels as they trailed from her collarbone to the center of her breastbone. *It probably cost as much as a car*, she thought. *A car? A house. A mansion.*

"A loan?" she suggested weakly.

He shook his head. "A gift."

Irene had never seen anything so lavish and exquisite as this necklace, and knew she never would again. Crazy to think she was wearing a million euros around her neck—or more—when she had less than twenty euros in her purse.

But it wasn't a gift, whatever Sharif had said. It was payment in advance. No man gave something for nothing. What was the difference between accepting a diamond necklace from a sheikh or getting a hundred bucks from old Benny who pumped gas as the Quick Mart? No difference at all.

But she found herself still stroking the jewels for another five minutes before she gathered the willpower to reach for the clasp.

He put his larger hand over hers, stopping her. Their eyes met in the mirror.

"They're yours."

"I told you. I can't accept."

"I won't take them back. They were bought for you today in Rome."

"Rome?" she cried. "How?" Then she remembered his newspaper. "It's very wasteful," she grumbled. "Sending private jets all around the world at the drop of a hat. Buying diamonds for a stranger."

"You're not a stranger. Not anymore." He shrugged. "If you don't want the necklace, toss it in the lake. Bury it in the garden. I care not. It's yours. I won't take it back."

"But—"

"I'm bored with this subject. Let's find something fun to do." He gave her a lazy smile. "Perhaps go congratulate the bride and groom on their civil ceremony?"

Guilt flashed through her as she recalled how she'd barely spoken three words with Emma all day. "Good idea," she mumbled.

But for all the rest of the long afternoon, she found herself unable to take off the necklace, or to part company with Sharif, who was continually at her side, whispered shocking things to try to make her laugh, and then laughing himself when she whispered her own shocking things in return.

The beautiful, chic supermodel types goggled at them for the rest of the afternoon, and through dinner, too, as if they couldn't imagine what the handsome, powerful Emir of Makhtar could find so fascinating about Irene. Oh, if only they knew. She was insulting him, mostly.

She allowed herself a small, private giggle with her after-dessert coffee. Then her eye caught Emma's worried face across the table.

Irene's smile fell. Looking away, she scowled. Emma should know she didn't need to worry. She knew what she was doing.

Didn't she?

After dinner, alone in her own room for the first time that day, Irene looked down in awe at the beautiful gown Emma had loaned her for the ball that night. It was strapless red silk, with a sweetheart neckline and a very full skirt. The perfect gown for a night that would be the culminating event of the wedding celebration. Tomorrow would be nothing but hangovers and staggered breakfasts, as guests scattered for the airport, for the train, back to their real lives. But tonight—*tonight*.

Tonight there would be fireworks.

Trembling, Irene looked at herself in the mirror, wearing only a red strapless lace bra and panties—and the necklace. Lifting her long dark hair off her neck, Irene bit her lip, turning her head to the left and right.

She'd wear it just a few hours more. Then she'd give it back to Sharif, she promised herself, and no harm done.

Irene brushed her long dark hair, then piled the heavy weight on top of her head in an elegant topknot. She put on black eyeliner and red lipstick. Pulled on the strapless scarlet ball gown. Zipped it up behind her.

Looked in the mirror.

A woman she didn't recognize looked back at her.

Beautiful.

Exotic.

Rich.

An illusion, she thought. Just for tonight. Tomorrow she'd turn back into a pumpkin. She'd face the hollow choice of asking a friend for a job, against her pride and principles, or else going back to Paris to pack her things to return to Colorado, a penniless failure. She'd go back with nothing but the dream that someday, if she worked hard enough and followed all the rules, she'd be good enough. She'd find a good man to love her as she wanted to be loved. She took a deep breath.

But just for tonight, she would forget all that. She'd pretend she was someone else, just like the other women at the villa, wealthy and beautiful and without a care in the world.

Going out into the hall, Irene ducked back when she saw Emma and Cesare, both of them dressed for the ball, coming out of the next doorway. Emma was giving her husband an impish smile as she ran her hand down the front of his tuxedo. Cesare looked at her with a low growl, then gave her a passionate kiss, pulling her right back into their bedroom—next door.

Well, that was one mystery solved. Sharif wasn't the one who'd kept her awake last night with all the noise. Smiling to herself, Irene counted to ten to give Emma and Cesare time to close their bedroom door before she went back into the hall.

She felt strangely nervous as she went down the sweeping stairs to the ballroom. Her hands were trembling for some reason she couldn't imagine. She touched the diamond necklace again, as if it was some kind of good-luck charm.

Just for tonight, she repeated to herself. *No harm done.*

The gilded ballroom was packed with people. Already, the hum of excited conversation and the music of the orchestra filled the huge room all the way to the high ceilings and the enormous crystal chandeliers. Unlike most of the weekend, which had involved an intimate number of twenty or so guests, tonight's event had brought celebrities and royalty and tycoons and politicians and billionaires, not just from Europe but also from South America and Asia and Africa. There had to be at least five hundred people, or maybe eight hundred. She had a hard time counting, and anyway, she didn't really care, because even though she wouldn't admit it to herself, there was only one person she was really looking for—

"Irene." His low voice behind her caused a thrill of pleasure to rush through her body. "You dazzle me."

Turning with a smile, she got her first look

at Sharif in a tuxedo and her heart lifted to her throat. How could he look even more devastatingly handsome? How was it even possible?

Taking her hand in his, Sharif bent and kissed her skin. At the touch of his lips on her hand, the hint of his hot breath, a flush of heat covered her body. Her eyes were wide as he straightened. He smiled at her, then held out his arm.

"Shall we show them how it's done?"

This time, there was absolutely no hesitation before she took his arm. They walked into the ballroom together. Irene was conscious of many pairs of eyes on them as they danced and danced and drank champagne and toasted the happy couple and danced some more. All night, they never left each other's side. They spoke about everything and nothing, and as she smiled up at him, he looked down at her, caressing her with his eyes.

Every word, every moment, seemed filled with magic and a delicious sort of tension, as if the very night were holding its breath. Irene felt dizzy, drunk with happiness. Against her will, she found herself wondering what it would be like to be in Sharif's arms, not just for these few hours, not just for this one night, but for tomorrow as well, and the day after that.

As they swayed to the music on the dance floor, he gave her a sensual smile, brushing an errant tendril of dark hair from her face. Just feeling the soft brush of his fingertips, even though they were in the middle of the ballroom with hundreds of couples around them, made her almost forget to dance. She stumbled, but he caught her smoothly, lowering her into a dip.

"Thank you," she whispered breathlessly, looking up at him.

Sharif's eyes were dark with heat. "My pleasure."

It seemed like minutes or hours that he held her in the dip, almost horizontally, and she wondered wildly if this was the way he would look over her in bed. Her knees went wobbly, but before she could collapse completely, he pulled her back upright, tight against his hard body.

She licked her lips, pressing her cheek to the shirt of his tuxedo. She could feel his warmth beneath the fabric, feel the power and strength of his body towering over her own. She thought she could hear his heartbeat.

He stopped dancing. Took a ragged breath.

"Irene," he said in a low voice.

Terror struck her—or maybe it was excitement—she no longer knew the difference. She only knew what was about to happen and that she could not stop it, even if she wanted to. And she didn't. Slowly, she pulled away from his chest. She lifted her gaze to his.

Sharif's eyes seemed to burn with dark fire. He

ran his hands over her bare shoulders, softly down her back. She felt the roughness of his hands, the size of them, the strength. He ran his fingertips up her arms, to her neck. He stroked the edge of his thumb softly against her aching lips, sizzling where he touched, making her yearn, making her *need*.

Cupping her face, he tilted back her head. She felt the warmth of his breath. Felt the hard heat of his body against hers. For an instant, time seemed suspended. She forgot the people around them. Forgot to dance. Forgot all rational thought. Forgot to breathe.

He lowered his mouth to hers, and kissed her.

It was like nothing she'd ever experienced. The memory of Carter's sloppy kisses of two years ago instantly evaporated, became laughable. Sharif took command, holding her in his arms, his lips hard and hot and sweet and soft. The music stopped. She heard only the rush of blood through her veins, making her dizzy, lost in the riptide of pleasure that tore through her, body and soul, leaving her weak and clutching his shoulders as if only this kiss could save her. As if his kiss were life itself.

She wanted him. She wanted this powerful billionaire sheikh, who had become simply Sharif to her. She wanted him. Even if it destroyed her...

"Fireworks! Come out now for the fireworks!"

The words rang out multiple times, in multiple languages. Irene heard the delighted response of the crowd, felt the rush as people started to leave the ballroom. Sharif pulled away. Her eyes opened slowly. She felt almost bewildered as she looked up at his handsome face, at his dark eyes, half-lidded with desire. Then she saw something else in his eyes.

Smugness. Masculine smugness.

She blinked. Took a deep breath. Eyes wide, she put her hand to her forehead.

"What are you doing to me?" she whispered.

"Don't you know?" Sharif tilted his head as he looked down at her, his black eyes hot with desire. He stroked her cheek. "I am seducing you, Irene."

A shock of awareness blasted over and through her, causing prickles to go up and down her body from her earlobes to her breasts and lower still. "You're—you're *seducing* me?"

"Forget the fireworks outside." Running his hands down the bare skin of her shoulders above her strapless red gown, he lowered his head to her ear. "Come back to my suite and we'll have our own."

He pulled back from her, and she saw in his face that he expected her to say yes. He thought he'd won. In spite of all her protests, he'd always expected to win. Dawning horror rose inside her soul.

"All of our time together—it's just been one long set-up? From the moment we met?"

Sharif twirled a tendril of her long dark hair around his finger. "I've never had to work so hard for any woman. But no woman has ever intrigued me more. Come back to my room, Irene. Let me show you everything the night can be…"

Irene ripped out of his arms, pressing her hands against her temples. *One long set-up.* All the laughter and banter. All the camaraderie and delight. She'd thought it was magic. She hadn't seen the secret work of the magician pulling the strings.

"It was all just to get me into bed?" she whispered. "All our—our friendship was a lie?"

Sharif's smug expression disappeared.

"Not a lie," he said sharply. "A seduction. Surely even you can see the difference."

"Even me?" Pain wrenched through her, the pain of shattered dreams, dreams she should have known better to have but that she'd allowed herself to believe in anyway. "Stupid. Stupid," she whispered, hating herself.

"Irene…"

Looking up at him, she hated him even more. She couldn't bear to meet his black gaze that always saw through her soul. Was he seeing through her now? Did he know what a fool he'd nearly made of her—the fool she'd nearly made of herself, letting herself fall into the magic, believing it to be real?

A sob lifted to her throat. Turning on her heel, she fled the empty ballroom, out into the night.

Outside, hundreds of wedding guests stood across the terraces, their eyes lifted up as the first explosions of colorful fireworks streaked across the sky, across the black mirror of the lake.

Irene fled in the opposite direction, toward the garden, her red silk skirts flying behind her. Only when she was in the dark quiet of the overgrown trees did she exhale. And cover her face with her hands.

She remembered how harshly she'd judged her mother and sister for falling for men's lines, again and again, first for love, then for attention and finally for money. Oh, if only she'd known how it all started! With such breathless, foolish hope!

Sharif's voice was low behind her. "I don't understand."

Trembling, she whirled around.

The moon had gone behind the clouds and in the darkness of night, she couldn't see his face. "It's been fun, hasn't it?" he said. "Why are you reacting like this?"

Fireworks suddenly lit up the sky again, and she saw his face. He looked bewildered. He had no idea what he'd done to her.

Irene was glad for that, at least. She looked

down, waiting for the sky to grow dark. Waiting for her voice to grow steady enough for her to speak.

"It's just sex," Sharif said. "It doesn't mean anything."

"It does to me," she said. "Either it's making love with all your heart, or else it's just an empty, hollow shell of what it's meant to be."

He snorted. "You're making a big deal out of—"

"I've waited my whole life for the man I will love. The man I'll marry."

Another boom of fireworks, a distant happy cry from the crowd, and she saw the shocked expression on his face. "You can't be saying what I think you're saying."

She waited for it to be dark again. Then she said quietly, "When I marry, it will only be for love. And our wedding night will be truly about making love. The kind that will last forever..." Her throat caught. "You've accused me of being romantic," she said softly, blinking fast. "I'm just waiting for the One."

"One at a time?" he said weakly.

She shook her head. He scowled.

"What difference does the number of lovers make?"

"To you, it doesn't." Irene looked up. "But it matters to me. Sex is sacred. It's a promise without words. A promise I'll only make to the man who will love me for the rest of his life, and I can love for the rest of mine." Her throat ached as she asked him a question to which she already knew the answer. "Are you that man, Sharif?"

A last blast of fireworks ricocheted across the night like a lightning storm, illuminating his expressionless face.

"No," he said dully.

The ache in her throat now felt like a razor blade. She forced herself to ignore it. To smile. "I didn't think so." Unclasping the necklace was suddenly easy. She blinked fast, and was proud of herself for her clear, unwavering voice as she said, "Thank you for a weekend I'll never forget."

Reaching for his hand, she pressed the heavy diamond necklace against his palm. He looked down.

"It was a gift," he said.

Past his ear, she saw movement on the edge of the garden, his bodyguards hovering at a distance. It almost made her laugh. "Your minders are here." With a deep breath, she reached up and touched his rough cheek. "I wish all kinds of beautiful things for you, Sharif." She tried to smile. "There's lots of magic to believe in. The kind people make for themselves."

But as Irene looked at his stricken black eyes, her throat suddenly closed tight. Without another word, she turned and ran toward the villa. Above her, the fireworks' grand finale exploded across the sky in exquisite bursts of color, like flowers blooming to life then just as swiftly fading away.

She'd passed the test. She'd won.

Irene barely reached her bedroom before her knees collapsed beneath her. Sliding to the floor in a splash of red silk, she covered her face with her hands, and cried.

CHAPTER FOUR

HE'D LOST. FAILED.

Sharif could hardly believe it.

I wish all kinds of beautiful things for you.

Remembering her lovely, anguished voice, he muttered a curse. He stalked through the crowd watching the last fireworks, stomping back toward the villa. Two bodyguards fell in behind him as always. One spoke to him in urgent Makhtari Arabic.

"Your Highness, you should know that—"

"Later," he bit out. His whole body felt tight. For the love of heaven, couldn't they leave him alone, even now? Stomping up the stairs, Sharif paused, looking down the dark hallway toward Irene's room. But what was the point?

There's lots of magic to believe in. The kind people make for themselves.

Furiously, Sharif turned toward his own suite. He could hardly believe that it was ending like this. That after hours of flirting with her, dancing with her, it had still ended with him going back to his bedroom alone.

For the last thirty hours, Irene had been the center of his battle strategy, the intense focus of his every thought. He'd used all his best techniques, the ones that never failed. He'd charmed her, listened to her, given her his complete attention—and not just for an hour, but for the entire day. More. He'd told her the truth when he said he'd never tried so hard before. He'd forced himself to seduce her slowly, an inch at a time, luring her as a horse trainer would tame a skittish colt.

And this was the result?

He looked down in disgust at the extravagant diamond necklace clenched in his fist. Women could never resist him. So how had she?

I've waited my whole life for the man I will love.

Sharif took a shuddering, incredulous breath. He'd never met a woman like this. She was crazy. But that was also why she'd drawn his interest, that light inside her. The fierce purity.

I don't fail, he'd boasted to her once. Well. He rubbed the back of his head. She'd certainly proved the truth of *that*.

What did he care? he told himself harshly. What was one woman to him, more or less?

He just had never failed before. Not in any arena of his life. When he tried something, he always succeeded.

Until now. And he suddenly felt something for Irene he hadn't felt for any woman in a long time.

Respect. No. More than respect. *Envy.*

Which didn't make any sense at all. After all, *he* wasn't bound by any antiquated, ridiculous rules about sex. He could have it whenever he wanted.

Well, except now. With her.

More irritated than ever, he stomped down his empty hallway. Four bodyguards were waiting near his door, glancing at each other, all of them looking nervous.

"Your Highness," one of them tried.

It took all of Sharif's self-control not to shout in the man's face. "Later," he growled, and pushed past them into his room, nearly slamming the door behind him. *Your minders*, Irene had called them. The symbols of a duty that in this moment chafed him almost beyond bearing. For God's sake, couldn't they leave him in peace, even for a moment?

In the dark bedroom, he tossed the ten-million-dollar diamond necklace carelessly across his desk, hearing it clatter and fall.

Then he heard something else.

"Your Highness," a kittenish voice gasped in the darkness. "I've been waiting for you!"

Irene? But even as the thought flashed through his mind, he knew it wasn't her. And if it wasn't Irene... Coldly, he switched on the bedside light.

To his shock, he saw the beautiful blonde Gilly, his sister's companion, who'd come from a respectable family with such excellent references.

"You sounded tired over the phone..." she purred, sitting up. She was naked, and smiling at him like a cat with a bowl of cream.

Sharif felt suddenly, crashingly weary. "How did you get past the bodyguards?"

"Oh. That." She giggled. "I told them there was an emergency with Aziza and I had to speak with you privately as soon as you left the party."

So that explained why they'd wanted to talk to him. His weariness faded, turned to anger. "And my sister?"

"She's fine," she said hastily, correctly interpreting his glare. "Well, except for counting down the days until her wedding."

"Counting down?"

"You know—with dread."

His jaw became granite. "Her engagement wasn't my idea."

"Yes, well..." Gilly waved her hand airily. "I'm sure it will all work out."

Turning away from her, Sharif sat on the chair by the fireplace and pulled off his shoes, one by one. He'd hired her as Aziza's companion only because, after years spent with an elderly governess, his young sister had begged him for someone closer to her own age. She'd been thrilled when

Gilly Lanvin had moved into the palace, with her sophisticated ways and intense love of fashion. But the result for his sister had been nothing short of disastrous.

When Aziza, at barely nineteen, had been sent expensive gifts and flowers by the aging sultan of a neighboring country, Gilly had turned her head with fairy-tale dreams of being a queen. His sister had begged and pleaded with Sharif to allow her to accept the proposal. Finally, with some reluctance, he had. It was a good match politically, and if his sister truly was so sure…

Except Aziza's certainty had now melted away as the wedding approached, and she realized she was about to become the wife of a man forty years older than herself, a man she barely knew beyond his excellent taste in Louis Vuitton handbags and Van Cleef & Arpels earring sets. She was desperate to get out of it now, but it was too late. Sharif had signed the betrothal. Some choices, he thought grimly, you just had to live with. He knew that better than anyone.

"…I knew you were hoping I would surprise you. I could tell." He realized Gilly was still talking, crooning in a really annoying singsong voice. "If you'll just come over here, Your Highness—*Sharif*—I'll rub you down, make you feel so good—"

"Get out," he said flatly.

She gasped. "But—"

"Get. Out."

Rising to his feet, he opened the door and spoke coldly to his bodyguards in the hall. "Miss Lanvin is returning to Beverly Hills. Get her last paycheck and put her on the next plane."

The bodyguards glanced at each other as if they knew they all had a good chance of being fired.

"Now," Sharif said tightly.

The next second, the bodyguards were at his bed, and as one of them lifted the naked, whining woman from the mattress, another efficiently covered her with a thick white terry-cloth bathrobe from the en suite bathroom. Within thirty seconds, they were carrying her down the hall and down the stairs and permanently out of his life—and Aziza's.

So the bodyguards were of some use after all. Sharif leaned back against his door, almost smiling to himself as he thought of using this point against Irene. Then his smile faded as he realized it was unlikely he'd ever talk to her again. The thought made him hurt a little inside. Why? Simply because he was too proud to accept failure? Surely he couldn't be so childish as that?

Pulling off his tuxedo and silk boxer shorts, he stepped into the shower.

Irene wanted to wait for love and marriage. So be it. Even if he didn't agree with her idealistic sentiment, he could respect it. He had no choice but to respect it.

His own life and ideals were different. When he married, love would have nothing to do with it. In fact, once he and his future wife had a child to be heir and another as requisite spare, he fully expected he'd avoid her for the rest of his life.

Climbing naked into bed, he gave a suspicious sniff. He could still smell Gilly's flowery perfume on the sheets. It irritated him. He was tempted to call the villa's housekeeping staff and have them change the sheets, but that seemed like more trouble than it was worth. Not to mention likely to cause a scandal. He could just imagine what Irene would say if she heard. Some scathing remark about the promiscuous nature of selfish, cold-hearted playboys.

Getting up, he opened the large oak wardrobe, found some clean sheets and changed the bed himself. He'd never done such a thing before, as from birth all of his needs had been attended to by servants. He'd mostly been raised by an American nanny and Makhtari tutors who taught him history and languages, along with fencing and fighting and riding. Even at boarding school, someone else had changed his sheets. So cleaning up after himself, even in this small way, was new. His fingers were clumsy as he did it.

Finally, Sharif stood back from the bed, surveying his work with satisfaction. Just because he'd never done something before didn't mean he couldn't learn the skills. Again, he wished he could show Irene. Again, he reminded himself he'd never see her again.

There's lots of magic to believe in. The kind people make for themselves. Her dark eyelashes had trembled against her pale cheeks.

Climbing into bed, he closed his eyes into a hard, dreamless sleep. He woke early, with the sound of his phone ringing.

It was his chief of staff, back at the palace. He was needed in Makhtar. His European vacation was over. No more pleasure. No more distraction. All that awaited him at home was cold hard duty and a young sister in tears at the mess she'd made of her own life. He'd have to find her a new companion to hold her hand for the remaining three months until her wedding.

Rising from the bed, Sharif yawned, rubbing the back of his head. He reached his arms upward, stretching his naked body before he dropped to the floor and did a few quick push-ups, just to wake up and get some of the adrenaline out of his bloodstream.

Find Aziza a companion? The situation seemed hopeless. He needed a woman who was both young, for Aziza's sake, and old, for his. He needed someone he could trust, someone who wouldn't jump into Sharif's bed, someone who would be professional enough to put Aziza's needs before everything else. Someone who…

Sharif's spine snapped back as his eyes went wide. He picked up his phone again. He read through business emails, made a few additional calls. Without hurry, he dressed in his traditional Makhtari garb and, leaving others to pack his suitcases, he went down to the breakfast room, bodyguards falling into line behind him.

He walked straight through the pale yellow room, ignoring all the women who tried to catch his eye. He offered an absentminded "good morning" to the host and hostess, then saw the person he'd been looking for. Pushing past all the rest, he went straight to Irene, who was sitting at the table with a plate loaded with pastries and scrambled eggs as she poured a great deal of cream into her coffee. He stopped right in front of her.

"I want you to come work for me," he said. "At my palace in Makhtar."

Irene's eyes still felt scratchy from a night of crying. She'd prayed she'd never have to face Sharif again. Foolish hope.

It had taken her hours to fall asleep, hours of running worried circles in her mind about the choice she'd make today. Would she take her first-class flight back to Paris, where she had only a few days left of paid rent, and then the open-ended economy ticket back to Colorado, to the rickety house on the wrong side of the tracks? Would she go back in penniless humiliation to the place where Carter had told her she'd never be remotely good enough for a man like him?

Or would she ask Emma to find her a job in one of her husband's luxury hotels around the world— using a friendship for her own financial gain?

In her darkest hour, Irene had bitterly regretted her pride, which had made her spurn Sharif's lavish gift of the diamond necklace. If she'd kept it, she and her family could have been wealthy— set for life!

But at what cost?

No. She'd done the right thing. He'd made her want him. Dazzled her with romance. But she'd resisted the temptation, and she'd never see him again. So the damage wouldn't be permanent, either to her heart, or to her soul.

So how could she abandon her principles now, and ask Emma to arrange a job for her?

But how could she not?

Anxious and unsure, feeling exhausted and alone with her heart still aching over the cold-hearted way Sharif had tried to seduce her, the way he'd *kissed* her, Irene had finally gotten out of bed. She'd taken a shower and dressed. No fancy designer clothes this time, but her own plain cotton T-shirt and hoodie and jeans fit for traveling. Going down to the breakfast room, she'd filled her plate with a mountain of food. She'd numbly sat down alone at the table.

Then she'd felt a shiver of awareness behind her. Without turning, she knew who'd just come into the breakfast room. A dark shadow came across the table in front of her.

"I want you to come work for me. At my palace in Makhtar."

It was the same husky voice that had haunted her dreams. Irene looked up from her plate of food. A shiver went through her body as she met Sharif's dark eyes, a hard aching tingle across her lips, which he'd bruised every bit as thoroughly as her heart.

He was once again dressed in his full sheikh regalia, with his bodyguards hovering behind him, the full presence of the Emir of Makhtar. And he'd never looked so handsome. The ultimate male figure of every woman's romantic fantasy. Or at least hers.

Wrong, she told herself fiercely. Her ultimate fantasy was a smart, funny, loyal man who would mow the lawn of their little cottage, read books to their children and love her forever. A man who would notice if a little neighbor child walked past the house, crying after her first day of school. A man who would roll up the sleeves of his old shirt, pull down his cap and go up to the school to make sure it never happened again. Her mother hadn't done it. She'd never known her father, either. Irene had been an accident, a mistake. Her mother had told her that all her life. *Stupid condom didn't work. Don't know which one.*

But after the first day of kindergarten, Dorothy Abbott had been the mother who'd comforted her, Bill Abbott the father who'd protected her. *That* was the house Irene wanted to live in. The parents she would someday give her own children.

There would be no accidents. Because until she met the right man, there would be no sex. No matter how she might be tempted.

"Work for you?" Irene repeated. She hated the weak sound of her voice and tossed her head, intending to give a sharper retort along the lines of *Immature as you are, your worshipfulness, I don't think you exactly need a nanny,* then she remembered all the eyes upon them. That type of banter was private, between her and Sharif, not between Irene Taylor, the American nanny, and the Emir of Makhtar. The banter was in the past, anyway. It was when Sharif had wanted to seduce her, and when she'd nearly given him the chance.

"I was not aware you had any children, Your Highness," she said coldly.

A half smile twisted the edges of Sharif's lips. She had the feeling he knew exactly how she'd felt forced to choke back her real reaction. He'd probably set up this meeting in public for exactly those reasons, damn him.

"I have a younger sister," he said.

Her lips parted. She tried to keep her expression impassive as she said, "Tell me about the position," as coolly as if she had already had five job offers today and fifty thousand dollars in the bank.

He lifted a dark eyebrow. "I would be pleased to give you further details, Miss Taylor. Shall we talk outside?"

She nodded. Rising to her feet, she followed him out of the villa, to the very same terrace where they'd first danced. It already seemed so long ago.

The blue skies and warm autumn sun had evaporated. Winter, too long held at bay, had finally arrived full force into northern Italy. The lowering sky was gray, and mist covered the tips of the distant hills across the lake. A cold blast of wind made her shiver in her comfy pink hooded sweatshirt and old jeans.

Irene looked pointedly at the bodyguards who'd followed them outside. With a sigh, Sharif gave them a glance, and they backed up to the villa wall, out of earshot.

"Why are you asking me to work for you?" she hissed. "What kind of trick is this?"

"No trick." He tilted his head, his eyes dark.

"I've recently had reason to sack my sister's current companion."

"What happened? Let me guess. You fired her for talking back? If that's the case, there's no point hiring me. You know that I—"

"She showed up here last night. In my bed."

Her cheeks went pink. "Oh," she said faintly. "Delivery service. How nice for you."

"No," he said sharply. "I don't sleep with employees. I threw her out. Now my sister needs a trustworthy companion until her wedding three months from now."

"*Wedding?* How old is your sister?"

"Nineteen."

Someone else getting married so young. It made Irene feel suddenly ancient at twenty-three. "Why would you choose me?"

Sharif's dark eyes met hers.

"Because I feel I can trust you to look out for my sister," he said quietly. "And I know I won't find you unexpectedly naked in my bed."

He sounded so sure of that. He didn't know what turning down his offer last night had cost her. Irene shivered in her thin cotton hoodie, looking out at the gray lake. She thought of what was waiting for her in Colorado. What was waiting for her in Paris.

"When is the wedding exactly?" she said.

"Late February."

"And the salary?"

"Ah." He relaxed, tilting his head as he gave a shrug. "For a trustworthy person of this nature, you understand, no price would be too great."

"How great is great?"

"Name your price."

Name your price? That was something people said in movies, not in real life. "You can't be serious."

"Try me."

Irene licked her lips. Recklessly, she thought of a huge amount, more than a whole year's salary working for her previous families in either New York City or Paris. She opened her mouth to ask for that amount.

Then she snapped it shut.

She mustn't be hasty. She'd read in a book once that women never valued themselves highly enough—that they were afraid to negotiate salaries out of a fear of being turned down, or even more ridiculously, of not being liked. Well, she didn't care if Sharif liked her, did she? And he was making it plain she had him over a barrel. If there was ever a time to value herself highly, it was now.

She thought of what it would cost to send her mother to the best rehab facility in Denver. The cost of moving to a brand-new apartment in a brand-new city, of paying rent for the next five years so her sister could go to community college and never again be tempted to go looking for some sugar daddy in a bar. Irene thought of the cost of making sure none of them would ever have to go back to that sad little house by the railroad tracks again. A new life not just for Irene, but for her mother and older sister.

So she took that first number and exploded it, like turning a single-story building into a skyscraper. Taking her heart in her hands, she kept her face expressionless and looked him straight in the eyes. "A hundred thousand dollars."

"Agreed," he said, before she'd even finished the last word.

Oh, no! She'd blown it! The fact that he'd agreed so quickly meant she hadn't asked for nearly enough!

"Per *month*," she added quickly.

He gave her an amused smile. "Naturally."

"Fine," she said, wishing she'd had the guts to ask for more.

"Fine. I will have my people pack your things."

"Thanks, but I prefer to pack my own stuff. I already did it in any case."

"Of course you did. Independent and responsible as you are." He smiled again, and his dark eyes seemed to caress her face, causing an answering spark of awareness to light like a match inside her. Match? That match had been lit from the moment he'd found her standing alone at the moonlit lake that first night. It had turned into a simmering fire that was waiting at any moment to explode.

She wouldn't let it. She'd already passed the test, hadn't she? She'd resisted her attraction to him and for the sake of the three hundred thousand dollars, more money than she'd ever seen in her lifetime or would ever expect to see again, she would resist it again.

Fortunately, she knew he wouldn't pursue her romantically again. Obviously, he'd been just trying to amuse himself with a bit of slumming during his friend's wedding weekend, but they were returning to real life now. To his home country.

Holy cow. Sharif was Emir of Makhtar. He'd made her forget. Once they were in Makhtar, though, she'd likely never see him in the palace, not until the day he paid her. Likely not even then. Paying the help? He had people to handle that sort of thing.

"So when do we leave?" she asked awkwardly.

He smiled. "As soon as we say our goodbyes and get the suitcases in the car."

Two hours later, they were boarding his enormous private jet.

"So what did Mrs. Falconeri say when you told her you were coming to work for me?" Sharif asked as they crossed the tarmac.

Irene blushed. "I, um, never told her."

He gave a low laugh that was way too knowing. She changed the subject. "What's it like? Your home?"

"An oasis on the Persian Gulf. Sparkling new city, palm trees, a bright blue sky, warm, friendly people."

She looked at him skeptically. "I already agreed to the job. You don't have to sell the place like a tourist-board representative. I want to know what it's really like."

Sharif stopped, looking at her. "It's the best country in the world. I would do anything for Makhtar. Sacrifice anything."

His love for his country shone in his face. She'd never seen such passion, idealism, vulnerability in his dark eyes. She had to look away.

Fortunately, it was easy to find something astonishing to look at. The inside of his private 747 looked nothing like any of the flights she'd been on. Not even that first-class flight. The front cabin of his plane was wide and gleamed with light and comfortable white sofas and seats, with a bar on one side and a large flat-screen television against a wall. It looked like the contemporary interior of an expensive New York restaurant.

Overwhelmed, she sank into the closest seat. "I guess I should call you *Your Highness* now."

"And from this moment, you are Miss Taylor," he agreed.

Biting her lip, she looked out the window. As the jet's engine warmed up, to take them away from Italy and up into the clouds, Irene felt her heart grow suddenly lighter. Thanks to this stroke of fate, she hadn't had to give up her principles. And she'd never need to worry about money again. This would change everything for her family. Everything. With a deep breath, she looked at Sharif.

"Thank you for hiring me," she said softly.

As the bodyguards trailed past him to the rear cabin, he frowned in surprise. "Thank you for solving my problem."

A flight attendant, glamorously attired in a skirt suit and a jaunty blue hat and scarf, served some sparkling water on a silver tray. Taking a sip of the cool water, Irene looked at her new employer.

Sharif looked handsome and powerful in his stark white robes, sitting on the white leather sofa on the other side of the spacious cabin. Taking his own sparkling water off the tray, he smiled his thanks to the flight attendant. Irene sighed with happiness, leaning back against her own plush leather seat.

"I wish all the people who were mean to me in school could see this." A low laugh escaped her lips. "No one would ever have guessed I'd someday be companion to a princess of Makhtar. Especially with my grades in geography. I couldn't have placed Makhtar on a map." Irene wasn't a hundred percent certain she could do it now, but she kept that to herself. "Um, are you still sure about this?"

He set down his glass. His handsome face was inscrutable as he slowly looked her over. "Why wouldn't I be?"

Irene hesitated, feeling self-conscious. "I told you I have a bad habit of talking back to employers. Knowing the kind of woman I am, Your Highness, are you sure you really want me as your employee?"

"I'm sure, Miss Taylor. There can be no doubt." His black eyes met hers as he said huskily, "I want you."

CHAPTER FIVE

IRENE HAD NEVER flown on even a small private plane before, let alone the huge 747 that belonged to the royal house of Makhtar. But by the time the plane landed that evening, she was growing shamefully accustomed to the luxury that accompanied Sharif wherever he went. Even the stretch Rolls-Royce, and the attendant entourage of black SUVs for the guards, was starting to seem almost routine.

There was just one thing she couldn't get used to. One thing that was a shock to her senses, each and every time.

She looked at him beneath her lashes, in the back of the limo. He was busy now, speaking with a young man, his chief of staff, who'd met him at the private airport at the edge of the city. The two men were speaking in rapid Arabic, leaving Irene free to sneak little glances.

Gone was the darkly seductive playboy she remembered. Here, Sharif was the emir. Formal.

Serious. And definitely not paying the slightest attention to her. Telling herself she was relieved, she looked out the window, which was tinted against the shock of the hot Makhtari sun.

Makhtar City gleamed from the desert, like a polished, sun-drenched diamond in the sand. It was a new city, still being rapidly built with cranes crisscrossing the blue sky.

She saw prosperous people, families pushing baby strollers on newly built sidewalks to newly built cafés. It had to be almost ninety degrees Fahrenheit, from the blast of heat she'd felt walking across the airport tarmac to the air-conditioned limo. Very different from the chilly morning in the Italian mountains. But Sharif had told her on the plane that this was their winter.

"In November, people finally come out of their houses, as the weather turns pleasant. In summer, it can reach a hundred and twenty degrees. Tourists complain then that swimming in the gulf is like taking a hot bath—no relief whatsoever from the unrelenting heat." He'd grinned. "Makhtaris know better than to try it."

It sure didn't seem like winter to her. The hot sun made her want to rip off her jeans and hoodie in favor of shorts and a tank top. But on the street, both men and women wore clothing that completely covered their arms and legs. They didn't even look hot, strolling with their families. Irene still felt a little sweaty from her four minutes outside. It was way more humid than Colorado, too. She'd have to get used to it.

Still, there was something about this city, this country, that she immediately liked. It wasn't just the gleaming new architecture of the buildings, or the obvious wealth she saw everywhere—luxury sports cars filling the newly built avenues, lined with expensive designer shops and gorgeous palm trees.

It was the way she saw families walking together. The way she observed, on the street, young people holding open doors for their elders. Family was even more respected than money. The wisdom and experience of age was respected even more than the beauty and vigor of youth. It felt very different from the neighborhood she'd grown up in. At least the *house* she'd grown up in.

As a child, she'd wanted so desperately to respect her mother and older sister. She'd wanted a mother who would give her hugs after school, a sister she could emulate and admire. She'd wanted a family who would look out for her.

But by the time she was nine, she'd realized that if she wanted milk in the fridge and the light bills paid, she'd have to take care of it herself. She'd learned how to run a household from watching Dorothy, but sadly there was nothing she could do for her mother and sister beyond that. Any attempt she made to suggest a different career path just made them accuse her of judging them.

Now, for the first time, Irene would really be able to help them. No more just sending them bits and pieces of her salary that didn't really change anything. With such a huge amount of money as three hundred thousand dollars—or whatever was left after taxes—she could change not just her own fate, but the lives of the people she loved deeply, no matter how many times they'd broken her heart.

"Miss Taylor. You are ready?"

They'd arrived in a large, gated courtyard past the palace gate, filled with palm and date trees surrounding a burbling fountain. Sharif was looking at her quizzically.

"Yes, Your Highness."

His eyes widened at her meek, impersonal tone. But she knew how grand households worked. One hint that she was anything but his sister's companion, a single sly suggestion that she was also the emir's mistress, and by nightfall she'd be despised by the entire palace staff.

A uniformed servant opened the door, and she stepped out.

"It's cooler," she said in surprise.

"The palace is on the gulf. And here in the courtyard—" Sharif's eyes seemed to caress her "—you can feel the soft breeze beneath the shade of the palm trees."

She looked up at the towering Arabic fantasy of the palace in front of her, like something out of a dream. "It's just like you said it would be."

"The palace?"

"The whole country."

Sharif paused. "I'm pleased you like it." He turned to his young chief of staff. "Please escort Miss Taylor to her new quarters."

The young man looked at Irene with clear interest. "With pleasure."

Sharif stepped between them. "On second thought," he said abruptly, "I will do it myself."

"Yes, sire," the young man said, visibly disappointed. Sharif swept forward in his robes, and Irene fell into step behind him.

"You shouldn't have done that," she whispered once they were out of earshot. "You can't show any particular interest in me. The other servants will talk."

"Let them talk. I didn't like the way he looked at you."

"Friendly?"

Sharif scowled. "Flirty."

"And that is bad because…he's married."

"No."

"Engaged."

"No."

"A womanizer. A liar. A brute."

Sharif's jaw twitched. "No, of course not. Hassan is none of those things. He is an honorable, decent man. Of course he is. He's my chief of staff."

Irene looked at him from beneath her eyelashes. "So why not let him take me?"

"If any man is going to take you," he said softly, "it will be me."

She stopped, blushing in confusion. Surely he couldn't still be thinking he...

"Your room is next to my sister's. I am headed that way."

She exhaled. "Oh."

The palace was huge, with high ceilings and intricate Middle Eastern architecture. As they passed from room to room, each more lavish than the last, every servant they passed bowed at the sight of Sharif, with obvious deep respect.

So many rooms, so many hallways. Irene grew increasingly worried that she'd ever be able to find her way back again. After they went up a flight of stairs, she expected to see some sort of servants' wing. Instead, the rooms just got more lavish still. A sudden fear seized her.

"Your bedroom isn't in the same hallway as mine, is it?"

Sharif looked down at her with his inscrutable black eyes. "Why, Miss Taylor," he said softly, "are you asking for directions to my room?"

"Yes—I mean, no! I mean..."

He tilted his head. After a full day since his

morning shave, there was a dark shadow along his sharp jawline that made him seem even more powerfully masculine. "Your room is close to mine. That won't be a problem, I presume?"

She licked her lips. "I'm not sure that's a good idea."

"Why?"

Because part of her was still afraid she might forget herself some night and sleepwalk naked into his bed, just like hapless What's-her-name who got fired. If Sharif knew the hot dreams she'd had last night, starring him… And he was her *employer* now.

Irene shook her head helplessly. "I just wouldn't want you to think…"

He paused, his sensual lips curved as he looked down at her, close but not touching. "Think what, Miss Taylor?"

Her voice came out in an embarrassing little squeak. "Never mind."

Sharif stared at her for a long moment, then setting his jaw, he turned away with a swirl of robes. "This way."

She followed him down the new hallway, still shaking with the ache of repressed desire. As they went down the marble halls and approached the royal apartments within the palace, the hallways grew more crowded, not just with servants, but also with the emir's advisers, serious men all in white robes, some of whom bowed as Sharif passed, others who merely inclined the tip of their heads. But in the faces of them all, Irene saw the most sincere respect.

"They love you," she said.

He glanced at her. "Don't sound so surprised," he said dryly.

"It's just that—I don't see respect like this for leaders anymore."

His jaw tightened. "They just remember how it was. Before."

"Before?"

"Here we are, Miss Taylor." His voice had gone cold and formal again. He pushed open a door, giving only a brief glance inside before he indicated she should go forward, while he waited in the hall.

Irene stepped into the room.

"Oh," she gasped. She took two steps inside, looking at the enormous bed, the view over the Persian Gulf, complete with her own balcony. The lavishness of the Middle Eastern decor was like nothing she'd ever seen before. She'd thought her room at the Falconeri villa in Lake Como had been spectacular, but it had been like a roadside motel room, compared to this!

"This whole room is for me?" she said faintly.

Sharif did not enter the room.

"Dinner is at nine."

She turned back to face him, her cheeks flooded with heat as, against her will, she immediately pictured an intimate dinner for two, with total privacy. "I don't know if—"

"My sister will be joining us."

"Oh." Her blush deepened. "Then of course I will be there."

"Of course, since I bid it." His voice reminded her of her place here, and who was king. But his sensual dark eyes said something else.

She had to get a hold of herself!

"Thank you, Your Highness. I look forward to meeting my new charge."

With an answering bow of his head, he left her.

Irene closed the door behind her, sagging back against it as she exhaled. Then she looked slowly around her incredible bedroom. It was twice as big as the whole *house* she'd grown up in. She looked at the silk damask, the fanciful decorations, the gold leaf on the walls. And most surprising of all: her meager possessions from her rented studio apartment in Paris had miraculously been transported here. How the heck had he done that? What was he, magic?

Well. Yes.

If not magic, he was a magician who knew well how to pull invisible strings.

But they had a deal. A business arrangement. Her whole family's future was now riding on it.

She couldn't forget that. One slip-up, one indication that she was still desperately fighting her attraction to him—now more than ever—and she'd be thrown out as ruthlessly as her predecessor.

She just had to forget everything that had happened in Italy, that was all. Forget the heat of his skin on hers when he'd taken her hand. Forget his smile. The intensity of his dark eyes. The strength of his body against hers as he'd swayed her to the music. Forget the passion of the kiss that had set her on fire.

She had to forget the huskiness of his voice as he said, *I am seducing you, Irene.*

The Emir of Makhtar, powerful billionaire, absolute ruler of a wealthy Persian Gulf kingdom, had once wanted her—a plain, simple nobody. She had to forget that miracle. *Forget it ever happened.*

Irene put a tremulous hand to her bruised, tingling lips, still aching from his kiss the night before.

But how could she?

Sharif paced three steps across the dining hall.

Irene was late. It surprised him.

So was his sister, but that left him less surprised. He'd briefly spoken with Aziza earlier, after showing Irene—*Miss Taylor*, he corrected himself firmly—to her room. His sister had been glad to see him for about three seconds, before he'd informed her, without explanation, that he'd fired Gilly and hired a new companion.

"But she was going to take me to Dubai tomorrow," Aziza had wailed. "Isn't it bad enough that you're forcing me to go through with this wedding? Do you also have to take away my only friend? I'm trapped here! Like a prisoner!"

And she'd fallen with copious sobs to her enormous pink canopy bed.

Irritated by the memory, Sharif paced back across the dining hall. He leaned his hand against the stone fireplace. It had been built nearly nineteen years before, along with the rest of the palace, in perfect replica of the previous building, which had been left in ruins during the brief dark months of civil war after his father's sudden death.

Aziza could blame him if she wanted for her choice to marry. But he would not go back on his word. He would not risk scandal and instability. Not for his own happiness. Nor even for his sister's.

He heard a noise and whirled around, only to discover his chief of staff. "Yes?"

The man bowed. "I regret to inform you, sire," he said sadly, "that I carry a message from the sheikha. She wished me to relay to you that she is unwell and will not be attending you at dinner, nor meeting her new companion."

Sharif's eyes narrowed. Irritation rose almost

to an unbearable level as he pictured his spoiled, petulant little sister coming up with this plan as a way to register her complaint and get her own way. The fact that it shamed him, as host and brother, that she was refusing to appear for dinner and meet her new companion would only make her happier still.

"Did she. Very well," he said coldly. "Please inform the kitchen that no meals are to be brought to her room. Perhaps if she grows hungry, she will remember her manners."

"Yes, sire," Hassan said unhappily, and bowed again.

Sharif watched him go. He'd told Irene the truth. His chief of staff would be a fine choice for any woman to take as husband—a steady, good-hearted man of some consequence, and at twenty-eight, he was probably even looking for a bride. And yet, when he'd seen the young man starting to walk Irene to her room, seeing them together had caused a strange twist to Sharif's insides. He hadn't liked it. At all. It had almost felt like—jealousy. A sensation he wasn't used to feeling.

His body tightened as he remembered how she'd trembled in his arms, when he'd seized her lips with his own. How she'd thrown her arms around him and leaned against his body, kissing him back softly and uncertainly at first, then with increasing force and a passion that matched his own. His one and only failure at seducing a woman. Ironic, since it was the one he'd wanted most. He still ached to possess her.

Sex is sacred. It's a promise without words. A promise I'll only make to the man who will love me for the rest of his life, and I can love for the rest of mine.

He pushed the memory away. He wasn't going to waste any more time hungering for a woman he could not have. He was bewildered by her idealistic decision, yes. But he respected it. And realized now why he'd envied it.

Because love, or even lust, would never coexist with marriage in Sharif's life. That pure lovemaking Irene had spoken of so wistfully would never be in the cards for him.

Few people have that anyway, he told himself harshly. *Lust is brief, marriage is long and romantic love is a fantasy.*

Turning away, Sharif lifted a silver goblet from the polished wood dining table. He took a long drink of cold water. He wiped his mouth.

Irene's nervousness around him, the way she held his gaze for longer than strictly necessary, told him she still desired him. If he truly wanted to seduce her, in spite of her romantic ideals—He cut off the thought. He wasn't that much of a selfish bastard. He would leave her alone. Let her go. Even after that searing kiss. Even though he wanted her more than he'd wanted any woman. He would not allow himself to...

"Sorry I'm late."

Irene's voice was breezy, unrepentant. It caused heat to flash through his body. He turned, but whatever mocking reply he'd been about to make died forgotten on his lips when he saw her.

She was dressed in white, the color of purity. Could her meaning be any more plain? But even if he knew what she was telling him, her plan had backfired. Because the white of her modest dress only served to set off her creamy skin. Her thick black hair looked exotic, her brown eyes mysterious and deep as midnight. She looked like a woman any man would willingly die for.

Her expression darkened as she looked left and right. "Where is your sister?"

Sister? He struggled to remember. Oh yes. "Aziza..." His voice was hoarse. He cleared his throat. "I regret my sister is not feeling well. She will be unable to join us tonight."

Irene glared at him suspiciously.

"Not my idea, I assure you," he said. "But if my sister is not hungry, I certainly am." The understatement of the year. "Come. I'm sure my chef is growing antsy, as his dinner has certainly been ready for a while now."

"Oh." For the first time, Irene looked uncomfortable. "I am sorry. I didn't think of that." She bit her lip. "But just the two of us—I mean, it doesn't really seem appropriate to—"

"To what? To eat?"

"Alone. Just the two of us."

"What would you like me to do to avoid gossip? Invite someone else to join us? Perhaps my chief of staff?" he said coldly.

Her eyes brightened. "Good idea."

He scowled. "Unfortunately he has other duties. He's already gone home to his family."

"To his girlfriend?"

"His mother. You take a great deal of interest in him for someone you just met."

She shrugged. "He's just the only person I've met. Other than the three different people I had to ask for directions to find the dining room, that is."

So that was why she was late. He'd thought she'd done it on purpose, to taunt him. He relaxed as the servants brought out plates of food, stews of chicken and meat, rice, vegetables and traditional Makhtari flatbread. The air around them suddenly smelled of spice, of cardamom and saffron. She sniffed appreciatively.

"Tell me more about your country," she said, digging into her dinner. "It is my home now, at least for the next few months." She took another bite of chicken and sighed with pleasure. "You said it wasn't always like this."

"No." He wasn't sure how much he wanted to

tell her. "If you are going to be companion to my sister, you'll be expected to know," he said finally. "When my father died, the country fell into civil war."

The color drained from her face. She set down her fork. "Oh, no."

"My father had held everything together. With him suddenly gone, none of the great families could agree on anything. Except that they didn't want a fifteen-year-old boy on the throne."

"How bad did it get?" she said quietly.

Gripping his silverware, he looked down at his plate.

"Half this city burned," he said. "By the time I arrived back here from boarding school, this palace was ash. One day, I was a boy studying astronomy and calculus and history. The next, my father was dead, my mother prostrate with grief and rage, my home destroyed. And my country in flames."

Silence fell in the shadows of the dining room.

Slowly, Sharif lifted his gaze to hers. He saw tears streaming down Irene's stricken, beautiful face. Strange, when he felt nothing. He'd stopped feeling anything a long time ago.

"What did you do?" she choked out.

"What I had to."

"You were only fifteen."

"I grew up quickly. My mother's brother, and

my father's former adviser, the vizier, were both trying to claim themselves as regent until my eighteenth year. They were destroying Makhtar in their battle. Even at fifteen, I could see that." Feeling that he wanted to finish the topic as quickly as possible, he set down the goblet. "So I made the deal I had to make to save my country. Then I brought Aziza to live with us. She was a baby, a newborn."

"She wasn't living with you before?"

"She was with her mother."

Irene frowned. "But your mother was with you."

"Aziza is my half sister. The day I lost my father, she became doubly an orphan. She lost both her parents."

"You can't mean..." Irene gave a low gasp. "Aziza's *mother* was your father's mistress, who killed him?"

He gave a single nod.

Her hands covered her mouth as if she couldn't bear the pain—but why? Sharif wondered, as if from a distance. It was not her pain to bear. Why was she taking it so personally?

"And you still brought her here? Raised her?"

"Aziza had been left with a paid servant. I couldn't abandon her. She is my *sister*." Setting his jaw, he looked away. His voice was thick as he said, "Nothing that happened was her fault. She needed me."

For a long moment, Irene looked at him.

"You have a heart," she whispered.

He set his jaw. "What else could I have done? Refused to even see her, as my mother did? Leave her to the orphanage or worse? She's a princess of the blood. My sister."

"You love her."

"Yes." No matter how Aziza irritated the hell out of him sometimes, Sharif could never forget the first time he'd seen her, a tiny baby crying so desperately she was nearly choking with piteous sobs. He'd never allow anyone to hurt her.

"You have a heart," Irene repeated quietly. As if she still couldn't quite believe it.

"Anyone would have done the same."

"Your mother didn't."

Sharif felt a lump in his throat. "Don't be hard on her. She'd just lost everything. She barely was able to look at me, either. Her heart gave out. She died a few months later."

"So you were alone—ruling the country—at just fifteen? With a newborn baby sister to watch over?" She shook her head. "How did you do it? At fifteen, I could barely manage a part-time job after school to pay our utility bills. How did you manage to pull your whole country back together? All alone?"

Here it was, then. The one thing she didn't know. The thing he'd been dreading to tell her.

The thing that he had been trying to force himself to face.

Sharif put both his hands against the table. "Because even then, I understood human nature." He wouldn't be a coward. He wouldn't. He looked at her. "I encouraged my uncle to believe he would have great influence over me, to make him give up the idea of a regency. And as for the vizier—to him, I made a promise." He said quietly, "I promised to marry his daughter."

Irene stared at him, as if she hadn't heard right. She blinked.

"You…" She swallowed. "You're engaged?"

"Officially, it has not yet been announced." He looked back at the water, wishing for something stronger. In the royal palace he respected his country's long custom and abstained from alcohol. How he wished he did not honor such niceties at the moment. He felt he could have drunk an entire bottle of scotch as he forced himself to say aloud the very words he'd been desperately trying not to think about for months. "But it is time for me to make good on that promise. Our engagement will be announced after Aziza's wedding."

"Do you—" She flinched, then whispered, "Do you love her?"

"It's not a question of love. I made a promise. I cannot go back on my word. Even though I might wish otherwise." He looked away. "When my time comes, I will make the sacrifice."

"*Sacrifice*. You speak of it as if it's a death."

"Because it is," he said in a low voice. "For these last few months of freedom I've tried to enjoy what pleasures I could. But even then, even now, I feel the bars starting to close in."

Irene stared at him for a long moment, and he saw her beautiful face struggle between sympathy and anger. Anger won.

"How could you?" she said. "How could you live like you do—Europe's biggest playboy…"

"My reputation as a playboy might be more than my actions truly deserve…"

"And all along—you've been committed to marry someone?" She rose to her feet, her face a mask of fury. "How could you flirt with me when you were promised to another woman? How could you try to seduce me? How could you *kiss* me?"

"Because I'm trying not to think about it," he snapped, rising to his feet in turn, meeting her fury with his own—except Sharif's anger was cold and deep and edged with despair. "Can you understand what it is like to despise someone to the depths of your soul, and know you'll still be forced to call her your wife? To have a child with her?" He paced by the dining table, his jaw taut as he swiveled to glare at her. "You asked why I was at Falconeri's wedding. I barely know the man! I went because…"

"Because?"

"Because I was trying to accept my fate!" he exploded. Turning away, he forced his voice to calm down, forced his heart to slow. He took a deep breath. "I went because I needed to feel like any ridiculous fantasies I ever had about marriage were wrong. I knew Falconeri was marrying his housekeeper for the sake of their baby. I thought, if I went to the wedding, I would discover the truth beyond their happy facade. I'd discover they could barely tolerate each other. Instead, I saw something different." He lifted his gaze to hers. "And I met you."

Looking at Irene's beautiful, honest, stricken face, emotion filled Sharif's heart. He found himself yearning for what he'd never known, and what he'd never have.

Their eyes locked. Irene's expression became sad, vulnerable, filled with grief. "How could you?"

He looked at her.

"How could I not?" he said in a low voice.

Tears streamed down her face as she shook her head. "Never kiss me again," she choked out, and fled the room.

CHAPTER SIX

SHE SHOULDN'T BE crying.

She had nothing to cry about.

Sharif—*His Highness*, Irene corrected herself savagely as she stomped up the stairs toward her room—was her employer, nothing more. So what if he'd kissed her in Italy while virtually engaged to another woman? It wasn't as if Irene ever thought they might be together. She'd lost absolutely nothing. In fact, she should be glad to be proven right—Sharif was every bit the heartless womanizer she'd first believed him to be!

Though maybe not *completely* heartless…

Can you understand what it is like to despise someone to the depths of your soul, and know you'll still be forced to call her your wife? To have a child with her?

No! She pushed away the memory of his hoarse 〈voic〉e and bleak eyes. She wasn't going to have an 〈ounce〉 of sympathy for him. She was *not*!

I made the deal I had to make to save my country.

Childishly, she covered her ears as she continued to rush down the hall. Things were right and wrong. Black and white. There were no shades or colors between. Only excuses. She wouldn't let herself feel a whit of sympathy. What he'd done was *wrong*!

Irene somehow managed to find her way back to her room. The dinner that had seemed so delicious was now churning inside her belly. She took a shower, brushed her teeth and caught a look at her face in the bathroom mirror. Her hand trembled as she set down her toothbrush. She wiped her mouth with the back of her hand. Then froze.

She still felt his kiss there. She touched her lips with her fingertips. She could still feel his mouth on hers, the way he'd claimed them so passionately as his own on that night of fireworks in Italy. She could still feel the way she'd kissed him back, with a lifetime of pent-up loneliness and need. With intoxicating hope.

Irene dropped her hand. She couldn't think about that now. Glancing out her window, toward the moonswept Persian Gulf beyond the palace, she swallowed over the lump in her throat. Whatever it had been between them—a lie? a dream?— it was definitely over.

Climbing into her bed in the huge room, Irene

pulled the luxurious sheets up to her chin. What would Dorothy have told her to do? She'd have said that Irene shouldn't sell her integrity, not for any price. She squeezed her eyes shut. She'd couldn't remain in Makhtar, under the same roof with him. Not now. She'd take the first commercial flight out of Makhtar City tomorrow morning, back to...

Her eyes flew open.

To where?

To her hometown in southern Colorado, to join her mother, drunk and bitter, and her sister, growing old before her time? She'd give up her new-found joy at the thought that she could take care of them?

Irene took a deep breath. No way.

She wasn't going anywhere. She'd stay here the rest of November, then December and January and part of February. She could do it. She had to do it. So the answer was simple.

She wouldn't be even slightly attracted to her dangerous, sexy, all-but-engaged boss. She'd look into Sharif's face and be cold, cold, cold all the way to her heart...

She thought again of his handsome face, his dark, bleak eyes.

Can you understand what it is like to despise someone to the depths of your soul...

She wasn't going to feel an ounce of sympathy. Why should she, for a man who had everything in the world, who was handsome, rich and powerful, the ruler of a wealthy Persian Gulf nation? The man had everything!

Except love. Or even hope of love, until the day he died…

Exhaling, Irene turned on her other side, squeezing her eyes shut. She would stay here and work, but nothing more. She wasn't going to think of him for another moment, except as anything but her boss. She wouldn't… She vowed, yawning. *Wouldn't…*

Except she saw Sharif standing in the moonlight on the edge of Lake Como, dressed all in black.

What are you doing here? she choked out. He was the last person she'd expected to see.

He turned. The silvery light frosted the edge of his dark hair, illuminating his black eyes.

Don't you know? he said softly, coming toward her. She shook her head. He pulled her into his arms, brushing back tendrils of her hair. His expression was different than she'd ever seen before. He looked tender, hopeful, yearning as he searched her gaze.

I'm seducing you, Irene, he said in a low voice. Their eyes locked. *I've been waiting to seduce you for all my life.*

Waiting for you…for you. The words echoed across the moon-swept Italian lake mockingly, like the plaintive cry of night birds, and each echo

caused a new twist in her heart, somewhere between ecstasy and grief, because she knew she'd
been waiting for him, too. But all the waiting was
in vain.

But why? Weren't they meant to be together?
Hadn't they been waiting in their loneliness for
the other?

Sharif's expression changed, became stark with
need. As if claiming her, he whispered her name.
She was breathless, spellbound, as he slowly lowered his mouth to hers.

Come to me, he whispered. *Be with me. Love
me.* With every syllable of every word, she could
feel the brush of his lips against hers, so close, tan-
talizingly close. His last two words were so faint
she heard them only with her heart.

Save me.

And at that, her soul could no longer resist what
her body hungered for. Wrapping her arms around
him, she drew him against her and pressed her lips
to his. She nearly gasped from the explosive sensation of his mouth against hers. She pulled him
down against her, sinking back against the soft
bed. Her hands twisted in his hair. She felt the de-
liciously heavy weight of him pressing her deep
into the mattress, and gasped against his lips. She
needed to feel more of this, more...

Wait a minute. An alarm went off in the back
of her brain.

Mattress?

Irene's eyes flew open. She suddenly realized two things.

First: She'd been dreaming about him on the Italian lake.

Second: She wasn't dreaming now.

Sharif's body was over hers on the bed. His weight on hers. His lips on her. So hot. So sweet. So impossible to resist…

Then Irene remembered why she must resist, and she pushed him away. Hard.

"What are you *doing*?" she cried.

"What are *you* doing?"

Sitting up furiously, she turned on the light on her bedside stand. Sharif was sitting on the edge of her bed in a dark shirt and trousers.

"I told you never to kiss me again!" she accused.

"You," he replied pointedly, "kissed me."

"Don't be—" Irene paused at the sudden humiliating memory of pulling him down against her on the bed, of pressing her lips to his. Oh, dear heaven, was it possible that she, while lost in her dream, could have—

Irene shook her head furiously. "You shouldn't be in my bedroom!"

"That's not what you seemed to think a moment ago."

"I thought I was dreaming," she retorted, then immediately wished she hadn't.

His dark eyebrow lifted. "Dreaming of me, were you?"

Her cheeks flamed with heat. "It's the middle of the night! What are you doing in here? Get out!"

Sharif rose from her bed, absolutely calm, as if what had just happened hadn't affected him at all—even while it had left her overwhelmed, humiliated, intoxicated and furious. Stupid dreams! She hated them all!

He took a deep breath.

"I need your help," he said quietly. "I need you to come with me. Right now."

She stared at him. "Have you lost your mind? It's—" she twisted her head to look at the elegant, nineteenth-century antique bedside clock "—three in the morning! I'm not going anywhere with—"

"My sister has run away."

Irene cut off her angry words. She looked at his face in the dimly lit room.

"Run away? Are you sure?" She narrowed her eyes. "This better not be some kind of joke—"

"Do you think I would joke about my sister?"

She looked at him.

"No." She sighed as all the anger went out of her, making her deflate like a balloon. Pushing her blankets aside, she stood up. Amusement flickered in his eyes as he looked at her long flannel nightgown, which went up to her neck and down to her wrists.

"Is something funny?" she demanded.

He cleared his throat. "Not a thing."

Sheesh, did no one wear old-fashioned night-gowns anymore? Apparently none of Sharif's lovers. Whatever. Irene liked it. A deliberate choice from all the tight knit camisoles and hot pants her mom and older sister used to lounge around in, on the off chance a current boyfriend might stop by the house for a booty call.

Irene lifted her chin, silently daring him to say something about her choice in sleepwear so she could bite off his head. Wisely, he didn't.

"Aziza took no bodyguards. Only her old nurse is with her. It might be innocent. It might not be. Either way, I need you to help me find her. Quickly. Before any of the servants notice. Because once they do…"

Biting her lip, Irene nodded. Although many employees in a large household were loyal to death and would die before they said anything, others would find the gossip too delicious a currency to resist telling at least a friend or two. From there, rumors would spread like wildfire. "But why would she run away?"

Sharif's face looked grimmer still. "*Why* is irrelevant. What matters is finding her. Quietly. Before the news gets back to her fiancé and the whole wedding is in an uproar."

"But why," she persisted, "would your sister run

away from her own fiancé? If I were planning to marry, I'd be counting down the days. Wild horses wouldn't drag me from the man I loved…"

"You are a private citizen. You have freedom that Aziza and I never will."

"But—"

"You don't need to understand. Just get dressed and come with me now."

Was it possible his sister wasn't keen on this marriage? But looking at Sharif's hard expression and the impatient set of his shoulders, Irene knew there was no point in asking. She'd ask Aziza herself, once they found her. "Give me three minutes."

He didn't move.

"Wait outside!"

"Three minutes," he warned her, "and I'm coming back in."

She believed him. As soon as he went out in the hall and closed the door, she flew to her closet, putting on the quickest clothes possible, a casual maxi dress and a jean jacket. She pulled her unruly dark hair into a hasty ponytail and grabbed her purse. Three minutes? She'd done it in two. She opened her door. "Ready."

He'd been leaning against the wall. He straightened, his face shocked.

Now she was the one to be amused. "Surprised?"

"I've never known a woman who could—" He

pressed his lips together, then said tersely, "You're different. That's all."

Not totally different, sadly. One of the things that had given her speed was that she didn't want him back in her bedroom. But even now, against her will, she remembered how it had felt to have his body on top of hers. How it had felt to twine her hands in his hair as she pulled him hard against her and kissed him so deep she never wanted to let go...

"Um." Her cheeks turned pink. So much for treating him only as an employer. She'd kissed him. Told him she'd been *dreaming* about him! Trying to pretend the kiss had never happened seemed like the best bet. "Do you have any idea where she might have gone?"

He gave a single abrupt nod, then gestured for her to follow him down the silent hall. Her flip-flops thwacked against the marble floor, so she took them off to pad silently in bare feet.

Once they were out of the palace, he held up his hand harshly. She froze, confused. Then she saw that the gesture wasn't for her, but for the bodyguards outside. For the first time since she'd known him, he was leaving all the bodyguards behind.

"Are we taking a plane?" she ventured.

Still walking, he shook his head. "It would involve too many people. I don't want to take that risk until I know what she's doing. We'll have to travel in a way that no one will look twice at us. In a way that makes us invisible."

Irene followed him across the gated courtyard, the only light the moon, the only sound the burble of the unseen fountain. He stopped in front of a building with large sliding doors. He paused, his hands clenched at his sides. She looked up and saw an expression on his face that truly shocked her to the core.

Fear.

She'd never thought Sharif could be afraid of anything. But she tried to imagine how she would feel if her sister had run away. If her mother was missing and unable to be found. The powerless fear that would grip her heart.

"We'll find her, Sharif," she whispered, trying to offer comfort. "We will. I'll help you find her." She reached for his hand. "Everything will be all right. You'll see."

For a moment, he looked down at her hand.

"Thank you," he said in a low voice. He pulled his hand away, the brief moment of vulnerability gone, the ruthless air of command returned, and he wrenched open the garage door. "Let's go."

"I still can't believe this is your idea of invisible," Irene grumbled a few hours later.

Sharif gave her a wicked grin from the driver's

seat of the insanely expensive red sports car. "Just trying to fit in."

"Fit in," she snorted. She stretched in the passenger seat, yawning. "You—"

Then she saw the bright skyscrapers in the distance. Her mouth snapped shut as her eyes went wide.

She breathed, "Is that—?"

"Yes," he said. "Dubai."

It was still early morning, and though the sun was barely in the sky, already it was growing hot. She'd slept through the first few hours of darkness, and had just a dim memory of a perfectly modern highway across bare, empty desert, and a sky that was inky black with stars.

They'd entered the United Arab Emirates at the Makhtari border, where they were welcomed with deep respect and courtesy that was fit for—well, a king; and yet with discretion that made it clear they understood this was not a state visit. Against her will, Irene had wondered if Sharif had done this trip before, and with whom.

They'd stopped for gas at a station outside Abu Dhabi. She'd gone inside and discovered the station was not that different from the ones at home. Same brand of candy bars, same sodas, same everything—except the labels had Arabic writing on one side and English on the other. Using her credit card, she bought a bag of chewy fruit candy and tucked it in her purse. She also got two coffees and brought them out to Sharif, who'd just finished refueling the flashy red car.

He'd stared at the outstretched paper cup, frowning, as if she were offering him jewels, not an espresso worth ten dirhams. Taking a long drink, he gave a sigh of satisfaction. He looked at her, his eyes deep. "Thank you."

"It's no big deal," she'd said uncomfortably. "It's just coffee." She tilted her head. "Aren't you used to people bringing you stuff?"

"Yes. Servants. Sycophants. But not—" He cut himself off. He looked at the coffee, then shook his head as his lips twisted upward on the edges. "It's not poisoned, right? As a warning to make sure I never try to kiss you again?"

She snorted, then gave a wistful sigh. "I can't really blame you for that. I'm the one who kissed *you* this time."

His eyes met hers sharply, and for a single insane moment, electricity crackled between them.

No! She would not let herself want what she could not have!

Turning, she opened the passenger door. "Your sister," she said.

"Yes." His voice was low. Getting back into the car, he started the engine.

But as they drove north from Abu Dhabi, she'd looked out the window, far too aware of Sharif next to her in the small interior of the sports car. She tried to focus on the gleaming buildings, the desert, the brand-new, immaculate highway with road signs written in Arabic, with English translations beneath.

Now, as they approached Dubai, Irene said, "How do you know she's here?"

"She was angry at me yesterday. For firing Gilly."

"Gilly?"

"Her companion who thought it would be amusing to ambush me while she was naked in my bed."

"Oh."

"Gilly was not a good influence on Aziza. She convinced her that things—luxury handbags, jewels, royal titles and money—would make her happy."

Irene leaned her arm against the window of the Ferrari and said sardonically, "I can see why that would bother you."

He gave her a sideways glance. "She convinced my sister to accept the Sultan of Zaharqin's proposal, because of his lavish gifts and high position. It wasn't my idea. But now I've given my word. I cannot allow her to back out."

"Nineteen-year-olds change their minds all the time."

"If my subjects do not believe my word is inviolate, how can I expect their respect? Their obedience?" Setting his jaw, he stared at the skyscrapers of Dubai ahead of them. "I suspected Aziza might come to our vacation villa here…"

"Vacation villa, huh? For when you're bored with being waited on hand and foot at the palace?"

"The guard called me a few hours ago. He confirmed that my sister's there, with only her nurse as chaperone. I'm grateful it wasn't worse."

"Nurse? Is she ill?"

"Nanny, I guess you would call her. Basimah virtually raised her."

"Why didn't she call and warn you what Aziza was up to, then?"

"Basimah?" He snorted. "She's protective of Aziza like a mother bear to a cub. She sees me as the enemy. Especially since the engagement."

"Hard to believe. So why has your sister changed her mind about the wedding? Did the sultan send her a gift she didn't like? Last season's handbags? The wrong color of jewels?"

He stared grimly forward at the widening highway, as the traffic on the outskirts of Dubai increased. He said reluctantly, "The Sultan of Zaharqin is older than she is."

"How much older?"

He paused. "Forty years."

For an instant, Irene just stared at him, wide-eyed. Then she exploded.

"You are making a *nineteen-year-old girl* marry a man *three times her age*? Are you out of your *mind*?"

"Aziza agreed to it. If she's changed her mind since, her duty is to serve her people," he said coldly. "Just as it is mine."

"It's ridiculous!"

"No, Miss Taylor." Sharif's eyes were focused on the road, but his jaw was tight as he said, "*You* are ridiculous to criticize something you do not understand. You have no responsibility to anyone except yourself and your own family. You do not know what it means to rule a country. It is Aziza's privilege and her duty to protect and defend all of our people. That means doing everything she can."

"But she is only nineteen—"

His hands tightened on the steering wheel. "I was fifteen."

"You grew up early."

"So did you." He gave her a hard, quick look. "You've spent so much time asking why my sister ran away. Why did you?"

She stared at him. "I didn't run away."

"You left your home, went to New York, then thousands of miles across the ocean to take a job in Paris. Then you traveled even farther to the Middle East. What else would you call it except running away?"

"I just needed a job…"

"You had a good job in New York. But you chose to leave, when a position became available working for your employer's cousin in Paris. It's not just about money. You wanted distance."

Her whole body went cold. If he already knew that…

"How much do you know about my past?" she whispered.

Sharif gave her a dark look.

"Everything. You think I would have hired you if I did not? I had a complete dossier on you before the plane even landed in Makhtar."

The chill in her heart became a freeze. "Then you know my mother and sister…" Her voice cracked.

"Yes." His expression changed, became gentle. "I know everything."

"And you don't—want me a million miles from your sister?"

He shook his head.

"But reputation matters so much to you—"

"*Honor* matters to me," he corrected sharply. "And you are not to blame for the choices others have made. Even if they're people you love." His knuckles were white on the steering wheel, and she suddenly remembered that Sharif, too, had good reason to believe this.

They drove in silence. Then he said, "The only thing I couldn't understand from the report is how you got that first job in New York. Why would a wealthy family on Park Avenue choose you from their agency, and send for you all the way from Colorado?"

"I was so young and from a small town in the West." She gave him a sudden impish grin. "They wanted a nanny with a wholesome, sheltered background."

He snorted, then sobered. "You are sheltered in your way," he murmured. "You protect your heart."

"Yes." Her smile faded. "And you're wrong to force Aziza to marry against hers."

Sharif's expression turned to a scowl. "With your beliefs about the sanctity of marriage, I thought you would support me."

Ahead of them, she saw gleaming skyscrapers, with futuristic architecture twisting improbably high, high, high into the blue sky. "Marriage isn't just a bunch of words on paper. The commitment can only come from your heart. From love."

Sharif's lip curled. He turned forward to stare stonily at the road. "Spare me your further thoughts on the subject."

Her cheeks turned hot. "Look," she tried again, "as ruler of your country, I understand your sense of honor, but surely even you can see that—"

"You, Miss Taylor, may lead your life however you want." He tossed her a contemptuous glance. "Make lifelong decisions based on romantic fantasies. Break engagements, marry on a whim, divorce as often as you like. You are free to make whatever self-indulgent, foolish choices you wish…"

"Foolish!" she cried. *Self-indulgent!*

"But my sister and I are not." He tilted his head coldly. "Tell me, Miss Taylor. How many happy marriages have you seen in real life? Can you name even one?"

"Emma and Cesare!"

"Too easy. They're newlyweds. Anyone can be happy for four days. Who else?"

She said slowly, "I was virtually raised by an elderly couple, neighbors who lived down the street. They were barely out of high school when they eloped to a judge's office, but they were married for over fifty years. They never loved anyone but each other. They raised children, they took care of each other, grew old together. They died one day apart…"

"After fifty years of marriage, they were probably happy to die."

"Shut up!" Irene shouted. "You don't know what you're talking about!"

"Oh, you can give out the truth, but you can't take it?"

"They loved each other! I saw it! Their house

was the only place I ever felt happy or safe in my whole childhood!"

Silence fell.

"Ah," he said softly. "At last. The reason for your ironclad virginity. You think if you hold out for marriage, you'll be happy and safe for the rest of your life. But it doesn't work like that."

"No? How does it work, then—sleeping around with women you don't even like, that you can't even remember? How is it working for you, knowing you'll never truly have a partner, someone to watch your back, someone to protect and adore? Tell me more about your great life, Sharif, how wonderful it feels to never love anyone, or have anyone ever love you back!" She shook her head, blinking away furious tears. "You're just scared to admit I'm right, because if you did—"

"Enough." He suddenly sat up straight, every inch the arrogant, untouchable Emir of Makhtar. His broad-shouldered anger filled the space of the Ferrari. "I've allowed your honesty, even appreciated it, because it serves my ends. I need my sister to have a companion I can trust. But do not speak to me of *love*." His low voice dripped scorn. "Love is nothing more than selfish delusion that weak-minded people allow to come before duty. Before honor. Before even their own good. People destroy their lives, and the lives of their families, over this poisonous thing that you call *love*."

The sports car seemed to be going faster and faster through the heavy traffic, until they were darting around the big trucks and luxury sedans on the road. Sharif turned the car off the highway in a hard right, barely slowing down.

He'd been right about one thing, Irene thought unhappily. Their flashy red sports car fit right in. No one gave it a second glance.

She took a deep breath.

"I told you when you hired me," she said shakily, "that you might regret it. Because I speak the truth."

"It's not truth. It's your *opinion*. One that you are free to have because you have nothing to lose. You do not have the lives of two hundred thousand people depending on you."

"No, but—"

"Share your feelings with me, Irene Taylor. Talk your head off whenever you want. But if you say one word of it to my sister—if you preach to her about love that lasts forever—that is your last day under my employment. You will be sent back home without pay. Do you understand?"

Setting her jaw, Irene looked away.

"Do you understand?"

"Yes." She gripped the edge of her leather seat as he turned the car sharply into a private driveway. Ahead of them, she saw a stucco fence at least ten feet high, with a guardhouse at the gate.

The air in the car, which had crackled with such sensual energy in the gas station outside Abu Dhabi, now seemed frozen over. How was it possible, Irene wondered miserably, that feelings could burn so hot one moment and so cold the next? Just a few hours ago, she'd been crying at the thought of his engagement.

Now, she would have dearly loved to push him out of the Ferrari and leave him in a ditch by the side of the road.

CHAPTER SEVEN

"I CANNOT BELIEVE that you would take such a risk coming here unprotected… Knowing full well that your future husband might hear of this foolish escapade…"

Sharif set his jaw, folding his arms with a scowl as he looked down at his young sister. He'd been lecturing her for some time.

"Of all the selfish, idiotic…"

Aziza sat meekly on an outdoor sofa on the grand terrace of their family's vacation villa, which overlooked an Olympic-size pool and the gleaming brilliance of the Persian Gulf beyond. His sister's eyes were turned down, but he recognized the stubborn set to her jaw. It matched the stubborn expressions of the two women sitting on each side of her.

Old Basimah was on the left, glaring at him with hard beady eyes, her sagging jowls quivering with unspoken fury that he, the elder brother who was merely and unimportantly the emir and absolute ruler of Makhtar, would dare to scold her precious charge.

Ignoring her, Sharif continued harshly, "You must never do such a thing again..."

But at this, the woman sitting on Aziza's other side, holding her hand, looked up sharply.

"She has explained why she came to Dubai, Your Highness," Irene said coolly. "She apologized for not telling you her intention, but surely you would not begrudge the sheikha a simple, discreet weekend vacation." Irene lifted an eyebrow, as if to say, *You, of all people, cannot criticize her for that.* When she saw her mark hit home, she relaxed and gave him a placid smile. "She is not, after all, a prisoner—is she?"

Sharif's scowl deepened. He'd expected that Irene would get along well with his headstrong young sister. He hadn't expected them to become friends so quickly. Or that she would take his sister's side so craftily, in a way he could not easily fight. Aziza knew it, too. There was a reason his sister was arguing in English, not Arabic.

"There are many places to relax," he replied through his teeth, "in Makhtar City."

Irene gave him a sweet smile. "But Her Highness had her heart set on coming here, where she could test her skiing lessons at the indoor ski slope at the Mall of the Emirates." She tilted her head. "She could have requested the use of your private jet, and flown off to a ski resort in Switzerland or Patagonia with an entourage. Instead, she came here simply and privately, at very little expense. Surely her thriftiness should be rewarded, not scolded."

The woman should be in diplomacy, he thought grumpily.

"Of course," he said through gritted teeth. She was not only giving his sister a reasonable defense, she was also obliquely pointing out his lavish spending on his own trips abroad. While not directly giving voice to her disapproval of Aziza's coming wedding, she was undermining his authority and giving his younger sister greater confidence in her decisions, to better fight him later. *Well played*, he thought. But Irene didn't know who she was dealing with.

Sharif looked down at his sister. Aziza's plump cheeks were still stained with tears, her hands listless in her lap. She was, after all, just nineteen. He himself had first started taking illicit weekends himself at that age as a way to escape from the pressures of the palace. That was what he'd first feared when she'd left—that she was meeting some boy here, some waiter she'd met, or heaven knew what. Thankfully, that wasn't the case. So perhaps—just perhaps—he was being too hard on her.

Sharif took a deep breath. "All I want is for you to be happy..."

Aziza looked up. "How can I be happy?" she cried. "When I'm just waiting, waiting to marry that old man?"

"How indeed?" Irene murmured under her breath.

Thus encouraged, the younger woman glared at her brother and tossed her head defiantly. "It's like having a date with the guillotine!"

Enough was enough.

"You made a promise," he said sharply. "You know your duty. You have yours, just as I have mine..."

"It's not fair! I went from an all-girls boarding school to the palace, and now I'm trapped there until I go to my husband's house, where I'll be trapped for the rest of my life." She shook her head. "You've lived your life for the last nineteen years, Sharif, bossing everyone around as emir, enjoying yourself in London and all over the world. What about me? When is my time to live?"

Sharif looked at the three mutinous feminine faces in front of him and felt momentarily outgunned.

He saw the tenseness of Aziza's trembling shoulders as she sat on the outdoor sofa. Saw the brittle expression on her face. All she'd wanted was a chance to swim and ski and distract herself from the engagement she'd entered into so hastily. He, of all people, could understand this.

"Perhaps in my desire to keep you safe, I haven't given you enough freedom," he said slowly. "I didn't realize you felt trapped in the palace, Aziza." He paused. "Shall we remain in Dubai for a few days? Have a holiday? Perhaps when you're done skiing, we should go on a shopping excursion."

"Shopping?" Aziza said hopefully.

"Every bride needs wedding clothes."

"How much can I buy?"

"Anything you want."

Aziza slowly rose to her feet, her eyes wide. "Anything? Five new handbags? A new wardrobe? Ball gowns? Jewels?"

"Anything and everything."

"Thank you, Sharif! Oh!" she cried, tossing her arms around him. "You're such a good brother!"

Now, Irene was the one to scowl. And he was the one to give her back a placid smile, as if to say, *Did you expect to win so easily? I've been in politics my whole life.*

"It's just what I needed," his young sister said, wiping her eyes. "It will make me feel so much better."

Sharif smiled at her. This was what he liked best—for his orders to be met with thanks and joy. But in this case, he felt he shouldn't take full credit. "Thank Miss Taylor," he murmured. "It was her idea."

Irene's lips parted. "It wasn't exactly my—"

"Thank you, Miss Taylor!" Aziza threw her arms around Irene's shoulders. "You're already so much more fun than Gilly!" A smug smile crossed the younger woman's face as she crowed, "Just wait until Alexandra sees all the things I'm going to buy today—it'll be twice as much as all the pictures she's been posting from her dorm! I win! I win, win, win!"

Irene rose heavily to her feet. Sharif saw the sour expression on her face and hid a smile.

He spread his arms wide. "I will have my driver bring the car around. My bodyguards arrived ten minutes ago."

"They did?" Irene said, then: "Of course they did."

Twenty minutes later, the four of them—plus a driver and bodyguard—were in a gray limousine, speeding from the villa to the mall, with the other bodyguards driving SUVs ahead and behind.

Sitting in the back of the limo, Sharif felt Irene's sideways glare. He didn't mind at all. Like his sister, he'd won.

Aziza was settling down, on track to a marriage that would increase the stability and prestige of his small nation. And, he hoped, her older husband would stabilize her. Yes, the Sultan of Zaharqin was older, but he was steady and respectable. It would be a good match. Something that would last, and would in time, as they built their family, lead to mutual respect, Sharif hoped, even affection, between husband and wife.

Stability. Peace. Those were the things he valued, both in his country and in his life. His eyes fell on Irene sitting across from him in the back of the limo.

He wished he could say he felt peaceful now.

They were barreling down the road at a breakneck pace, the driver well accustomed to the traffic laws of Dubai, which were often treated more like suggestions, really, than laws. The battle of wits between him and Irene had his blood flowing. All his senses were aware of her.

Sharif's gaze slowly traveled from the impatient tapping of her foot in those ridiculously casual plastic flip-flops, to the curvaceous outline of her body in the long knit cotton dress. A jean jacket covered her tightly folded arms in the frigid air-conditioning of the Bentley. He saw the angry set of her jaw. The warm creamy hue of her skin. She was staring out the window, her teeth biting down on her full, pink lower lip. She was clearly repressing the words she wished to say, but her body language said it all for her. She'd lost this battle, and she didn't like it.

He couldn't stop looking at her lips, the full

sensual lips that had kissed him so suddenly and unexpectedly when he'd gone into her bedroom to wake her. Her beautiful eyes had fluttered open, she'd smiled, whispered something he couldn't hear, then pulled him down hard against her on the bed. His whole body suddenly felt tight, his heart pounding at the memory.

What a woman. If it had been his choice, he would have chosen a woman like this for his queen, angry and sweet, sexy and idealistic and proud. He respected her. Even though it was a pain in his side, he admired the way she'd fought for his sister. Even before she'd met Aziza, she'd been protective of her. She wasn't afraid to fight for what she believed in.

He suddenly wondered what it would be like to fight with Irene every day, having her argue with him furiously over the breakfast table, her deep brown eyes shooting sparks of fire. Then taking her to bed every night, where the fire could explode. It wouldn't always be peaceful. Or stable. And yet it would be, because what was between them, both the good and bad, would always be real…

He cut the thought off. *Real*, he mocked himself. His lip curled. He was starting to sound as bad as Irene. Like a *romantic*. Real?

The promise he had made at fifteen to wed the vizier's daughter was real. His need to protect his

people and keep Makhtar prosperous and safe—
that was real, too. He would announce his engagement to Kalila as soon as Aziza's wedding was
done. Kalila would be his queen, would provide
him with the heir he needed.

That was the most real of all. Even if the thought
of what he'd need to do to get that heir on Kalila
repelled him. She was sly, devious, cold-blooded.
It would be like bedding a snake.

Whereas the woman sitting close to him now—

Irene made him feel warm all over. Hot to boil-
ing. She was passionate and alive. Everything she
believed, she believed with all her heart. She wore
her heart on her sleeve, even if that made her vulnerable, even if she risked looking like a fool. She
appealed to him in a way he couldn't explain, not
even to himself.

But the longer he knew her, the more beautiful
she was. Even now, when she was angry and tapping her foot with self-righteousness, she glowed
from within.

He wanted her. Now, more than ever.

Perhaps he'd been too hasty in deciding not to
seduce her.

Yes. He straightened in the backseat of the limo,
suddenly liking this idea. It was true he had a self-
imposed rule about not sleeping with employees.
Apart from the risk to the tranquility of his household, it had always just seemed, well, tacky.

But his position on this issue was rapidly evolving.

Just look how distracted he was right now, half out of his mind with desire. His mind was so filled with thoughts, his body so tense with need, that it was probably good he wasn't back at the palace, making decisions that affected the affairs of state. How could he be expected to make rational decisions in the condition he was in?

And Sharif was well experienced sexually. How much worse must it be for Irene, who was not? Every bit of her body language, from her tapping foot, to her teeth biting her pink lip, to her arms crossed tightly over her full breasts, told him that she felt the same overwhelming tension between them.

She wanted to remain a virgin until she was wed. Fine.

But how would she even be able to make a decent choice of husband, in the permanent lifelong decision of marriage, if she was half out of her mind with lust?

He could save her from the bad judgment that a mind clouded by lust could bring. Protect her from rushing headlong into a poorly considered marriage.

For her sake, he could seduce her. For her sake, and for his.

Because he wanted her too much. Even when

she was angry. Even when she was blunt. Even when she was annoying him with her wildly wrong ideas. Seducing her, taking her virginity freely given, would help free both of them from this—obsession—so they could each move on with their well-planned lives.

Though he nearly growled aloud at the thought of any future man touching her. He wanted to be her man. He wanted to satiate himself with her, to feel her lips against his own, to fill her, to suckle and taste and caress every inch until she gasped and cried out with pleasure and held him tight, so tight, as if she'd never let him go...

"We're here!" his sister squealed, jarring him from his thoughts. Blinking, he saw they were at the mall entrance.

"Skiing first?" he asked his sister. "Or shopping?"

"Skiing—definitely skiing. Then lunch at the Swiss fondue restaurant with the view over the ski hill..."

"How big is this mall?" Irene said, looking shocked.

"Dubai has the best and biggest malls in the whole world. Everyone knows that."

"Everyone," Irene echoed faintly.

Aziza turned back to him. "Your bodyguards can carry the bags while we shop afterward." She tilted her head, her eyes sparkling beneath her head scarf. "I intend to buy a lot, Sharif," she said warningly. "A lot."

He looked at her. "And I intend not to complain."

"Ah… This is the best day ever." The teenager sighed. Sharif looked from Aziza to the elderly Basimah, whose wrinkled face was almost smiling at him—surely the first time ever? Could a shopping spree really mean so much?

The limo stopped and a bodyguard opened the door. Cooing happily, Aziza and the older woman hopped out.

Irene did not move. She still sat glaring at him, unimpressed. Her foot, still crossed over her leg, was now tapping as if she wanted to do nothing more than give him a hearty kick right out of the back of the limo. "Distracting a teenager from a lifelong decision with a shopping spree at the mall? Isn't that like shooting fish in a barrel?"

"We all distract ourselves in different ways from things we cannot change."

"But she still could—"

"If she was mature enough to accept a proposal, she's mature enough to live with it."

Irene started toward the open car door, then paused just long enough to throw back a glance like a fistful of daggers. "I just hope you're happy."

A gust of hot wind blew inside the car through

the open door. Sharif inhaled the lingering vanilla scent of her hair, sensual and warm.

Not yet, he thought. A slow-rising smile lifted his lips. *But I could be.*

Irene floated on her back in the Persian Gulf, staring up at the starry night, feeling the warm water lap against her skin.

After three full days in Dubai, she'd seen everything, she thought. They'd gone to the top of the Burj Khalifa, they'd had high tea at a six-star hotel, the Burj al-Arab, shaped like an enormously high sailboat floating out in the water of the gulf. Now that there was no risk of scandal—now they had a story of "trousseau shopping" rather than "runaway bride"—Sharif made no effort to hide their presence. Yesterday, they'd taken a private helicopter to Abu Dhabi, where they'd met up with one of Aziza's friends from boarding school and enjoyed Friday brunch with their family at the British Club.

If the other expat families enjoying mimosas on the patio had been shocked to see the Emir of Makhtar invade their quiet club with his entourage, they, being British, had hidden it well and swiftly returned to the pleasures of the morning and talking with their friends.

So much for the sights. Most of the last three days had been spent on one thing: shopping, shopping and more shopping. Irene had enjoyed it at first. It had been a relief to leave the indoor ski slope, after falling on her face again and again in the man-made snow, feeling as ungainly and clumsy as an ox with Sharif's amused eyes on her. At least, she told herself he looked amused. Not smoldering. Not as if he was thinking, every time she fell into the snow, every time he took her hand and pulled her up, that he wanted to kiss her senseless.

Her cheeks still burned when she remembered how she'd kissed him back in Makhtar. Stupid dreams! Look at the trouble they got her into!

She'd tried to keep her distance from Sharif, keeping her focus on Aziza, as they went next to a different mall, where she saw a fish aquarium larger than a building, billed as the largest in the world. There were so many shops, people walking through them dressed in every way from tank tops and shorts to black abayas and face-hiding burqas. Although even they, if you looked closely enough, had high heels peeping out from beneath their hems, and carried ten-thousand-dollar handbags carelessly under their arms.

Watching Sharif buy so many things for his sister, Irene suddenly regretted she hadn't contacted her mother or sister for a year, other than sending them money from her salary. She bought her mother a floral tea set of bone china and a box of

baklava from Lebanon, and for her sister a tour-
isty canvas handbag with DUBAI printed on it
with big block letters and pink butterflies. She
had it all shipped back home. After buying herself a bag of tasty treats from the biggest candy
store she'd ever seen, she was done. Today they'd
gone to the Gold Souk, but as Aziza and Basimah
pawed through jewelry, Irene's feet had hurt and
she couldn't stop yawning. The other two women
had shopping stamina that put Irene to shame.

Even Sharif seemed to have infinite patience.
He advised his younger sister on her purchases
when asked, but always deferred to her choice.
Perhaps he wasn't a total disaster as an older
brother, she thought grudgingly. Even if he was a
total disaster for *her*.

Irene stretched out her body in the warm water,
letting all her aches and tensions dissolve, letting
her troubles float up to disappear into the soft,
humid, starry night. Strange to be alone out here.
She'd never imagined that she, Irene Taylor from
Lone Pine, Colorado, who'd had her lunch box
smashed her first day in kindergarten, and been
pelted with insults she hadn't even understood
back then, would someday leave that misery behind and live half a world away, in a glamorous
villa filled with royalty.

She sighed with pleasure. Aziza had gone up-
stairs to take photos of her haul to send to friends.

Basimah was having a cozy game of cards with the cook. Sharif had disappeared to make phone calls, presumably about affairs of state in Makhtar.

So Irene had pulled on her modest one-piece black swimsuit, wrapped her body in a towel and sneaked outside.

She'd meant only to swim in the villa's enormous pool. But as the sun had lowered in the sky, she'd found it impossible to resist the streaks of orange and persimmon light sparkling on the gulf. Would the water really feel as hot as a bathtub?

She'd looked around to see if anyone was watching, seen only the distant bodyguards and gates on the edges of the private beach. It seemed like overkill, in a city as bright and modern and safe as Dubai felt to her, but then everything about Sharif's security arrangements always seemed like overkill.

Though when she remembered his heartbreaking story about his parents, she could almost understand why he would go to such extremes for security. And why he would believe romantic love was either illusion, or poison.

Can you understand what it is like, to despise someone to the depths of your soul, and know you'll still be forced to call her your wife? To have a child with her?

Every time Irene remembered his bleak voice, she shuddered. Marrying someone you hated so much, sharing your life with them, your home, your children? It would destroy everything about Sharif. Everything that was, beneath his arrogant bossiness, so bright and alive. The marriage would be corrosive to him as acid.

The thought caused a hard pain in her chest. He would keep his honor. Maintain his country's stability. But at what cost?

Perhaps she'd discuss that with him, convince him that...

No. Bad idea. She needed to try to avoid intimate conversations, not encourage them. The last thing she wanted to do was feel anything more for him than she already did. She couldn't let herself see the emotion beneath his mask. She couldn't let herself feel his feelings, any more than she could reach out to feel him in her arms.

The Emir of Makhtar was not for her, and he never would be. Not in any way she could accept.

In three months, she would go home. She'd take care of her family, go to college. Maybe she'd be a teacher. She wouldn't give up on the life she wanted. Not for a momentary temptation, no matter how strong the temptation might be. When she loved a man, she would give him everything, or else nothing at all...

Lying on her back in the soft waves of the Persian Gulf, she looked up at the stars in the deepening night. If she turned her head one way, she could see the skyscrapers of the Dubai Marina towering overhead. If she looked the other, she could see in the distance the populated, man-made islands that were carved into the shape of a palm tree.

But here, floating in the water, she was totally alone, just her and the moon and the infinite stars in the dark, velvety sky. She closed her eyes, feeling the water caress her skin.

Then she felt a man's hands beneath her. Her eyes flew open and she saw the outline of Sharif's dark head in the moonlight, the gleam of his black eyes. Startled, she fell, putting her feet down in the sand and whirled to face him in the water.

"Sharif," she breathed. "What are you—" She caught herself. "I mean, good evening, Your Highness…"

"We're alone." His eyes burned through her. "You don't have to be polite."

She stiffened, narrowing her eyes. "In that case, I'll say what I've been thinking for the last three days. What the hell are you doing? Distracting Aziza with piles of cheap gifts…just so she can impress her shallow friends—"

"They weren't cheap, I assure you."

"This is her *life* we're talking about." Her eyes filled with tears. "She's too young to realize the choice she's making."

He stood in front of her, his muscular chest

tanned and bare, both of them swayed by the gentle roll of the water in the darkness.

"We become older by the choices we make," he said. "By the responsibilities we take—or don't take. You know this already. How old were you when you started taking on responsibilities for your family—responsibilities that should never have been yours? Was that your choice? Or were you just doing what you had to do?"

She felt the sandy bottom beneath her feet. The water was high—all the way to her chest, and up to his ribs. The water's gentle waves swayed their bodies. One hard wave could push them together. "We're not talking about me."

"We are now."

"You don't understand what you are making her give up. If she marries without love, she'll never be happy, ever."

"And you think you will?" He took a step toward her, his black eyes glittering. "You're so desperate to save your pure body for marriage. But how will you know the difference between love and lust, Irene? You who have never known either one? What will stop you from throwing your life away to the first man who makes your body come alive?"

Every inch of her body felt alive right now. She felt the waves caressing her overheated skin as she looked up at his handsome, angry face. She licked her lips. "I...I'll just know..."

"You *won't* know. That's the whole point." He looked angrier. "You need to be taught the difference. To understand. So you won't promise your whole soul and future away to some man who will never deserve it."

She felt his gaze fall to her lips, and trembled all over. Her mouth tingled, aching for his kiss. Remembering it. But as he started to move toward her, she stepped back in the water.

"Tell me about her."

"Who?"

"Your bride. What is her name?"

His handsome face was suddenly as immobile as stone. "I don't want to talk about her."

"But I do."

"What do you want to know, Irene? She is a poisonous snake who amuses herself with more lovers than drops of water in the sea."

"I know there's a double standard here, but have you considered your own long list?"

"It isn't her lovers. It's the way she relishes flaunting them. Telling me about them. She hates me even more than I hate her. She has—a cruel heart."

Irene's heart twisted at the thought of a woman like this being Sharif's wife, at his side, in his bed. She swallowed. "And this is the woman you want to be queen of your country? The mother of your children?"

His eyes looked dark. "Leave it alone."

"You think I might make a foolish choice in marriage because of lust?" she choked out. "Take a look at your own—because of pride!"

For a moment, she was afraid she'd pushed him too far. Then he looked away.

"It's not pride," he said in a low voice. "I am emir. I do not have the luxury of going back on my word, or offending Kalila's powerful family. I cannot take the risk of Makhtar falling into chaos, into war, ever again. You don't know what it was like." He looked at her, his jaw tight. "I would die first."

Irene looked at his taut shoulders. She thought of how few people she'd known in her life who would sacrifice their own happiness for the sake of strangers. She took two splashing steps toward him, then stopped, staring at his dark silhouette outlined by silver. His body was in shadow, illuminated by dappled moonlight, reflected from the water.

"Sharif." She licked her lips. "I have to tell you something. I…"

He seemed to brace himself. She exhaled.

"I'm sorry," she whispered. "All this time I thought you were a selfish playboy. The truth is you're…noble."

"Noble? No." He shook his head. "I'm just…"

"What?"

"Doing my job."

She felt a rush of admiration—even longing. She tried to push it aside. She couldn't allow herself to feel desire, attraction…infatuation.

"I always knew I would someday be emir. I've known since birth that it was my fate." He looked at her. "But you are free. You should enjoy it."

Free? She'd never thought of it that way. But in some ways, it was true. Sharif, as a billionaire emir, was a prisoner of his people—the servant and slave of his country. While she, who'd grown up with nothing, who'd had to fight just to survive, had always had one thing he did not. The knowledge that the choice of what to do with her life was hers.

"What do you want, Irene?" Sharif said softly. "What will you choose for your future to be?"

The question made her throat hurt. Looking down at the water, she took a deep breath.

"I want to have security for my mother and sister. I want to help my mother go to rehab. I want to be able to pay for my sister to go to college if she wants. I want what I've always wanted. To take care of my family."

"So we're not very different after all. You've made sacrifices, taking responsibility for the people you love, even at a cost to yourself. You and

I..." Cupping her cheek, Sharif said fiercely, "We are alike."

Irene looked up at him with an intake of breath. For a moment, they stood together in the warm, swaying waters of the Persian Gulf, their eyes locked in the moonlight. She felt his hand against her cheek.

His gaze slowly fell down her body in the black swimsuit. Beads of water glistened on the tanned skin of his bare, muscular chest. The tension between them changed. His fingertips trailed down her cheek, then moved to tangle in her wet hair. He tilted her head back.

And lowering his head to hers slowly, very slowly, he kissed her.

The kiss was different than any between them before. Slow, and lingering, and deep. She felt the silk of his lips against hers, so powerful and strong, their tongues meeting and twisting and tasting, tangling together, like their souls.

Their nearly naked skin pressed against each other in the sliding waves of the water, pushing them against each other, pushing them apart. She wanted him...oh, yes. And he wanted her. Everything he'd said about lust was true. In this moment, with her smaller body wrapped in his, she wanted all of him, forever and ever. She didn't think she could ever have enough. She wanted not just his body, but his heart.

She abruptly pulled away.

"You promised not to kiss me," she said hoarsely.

"I never promised that. You asked. Then you broke your own rule by kissing me yourself." He tried to keep his voice casual, but she heard the rough edge of his voice. "I still remember how you pulled me on top of you, in your bed."

Her cheeks went hot. "I explained about that—"

"Yes." His sensual mouth curved. "That you were dreaming of me."

"I never said—"

"I thought," he said, running a fingertip along her wet bare skin beneath her collarbone, "you were always going to tell me the truth."

She took a deep, shuddering breath.

"All right," she said in a low voice. "The truth is that I was dreaming of you that night in the palace. I was dreaming of you kissing me. And then suddenly you were there." She lifted her gaze to his. "It was the first time in my life that a dream came true."

Sharif's eyes were wide, as if he'd never expected her to admit so much. He said softly, "I would give anything to do more than just kiss you. If you'd give up the idea of…"

"Of being a virgin when I wed?" She took a deep breath, tried to smile. "It's not just about my body. It's about sharing the same level of commitment. In fact," she tilted her head, "I'd prefer for him to be a virgin as well…"

Sharif's shocked face looked almost comical. "You're joking, right?"

She shrugged. "I just have my standards."

"Impossible ones. Even as emir, even if I were free to choose, I wouldn't expect my bride to be a virgin."

"You don't expect to love her either, so clearly we have different ideas about marriage."

"Clearly," he said, sounding irritated. "I believe in reality."

"And I believe in dreams." Irene looked away. "There's a man out there, somewhere in the world, who will love me for the rest of my life."

"And if he never comes? What then?"

"He will," she whispered. "I have to believe it."

He looked down at her, their faces inches apart. "What if you're wrong?"

Irene shivered, feeling the heat and strength of his nearly naked body so close to hers in the night. She lifted her gaze to his.

"Then I'll be very sad," she said, trying to smile, "that I didn't sleep with you when I had the chance."

They stared at each other for a long moment in the moonlight.

"So that's it?" he said finally. "I can't change your mind?"

"Can I change yours?"

Wordlessly, he shook his head, and that was that. She exhaled. So did he.

Reaching out, he silently took her hand. He led her out of the water, splashing to the white sand beach.

He paused, looking at her. "A one-piece swimsuit?" His lips quirked. "A bold choice."

"You know I like modest clothes."

"Obviously so. Even Basimah has a bikini, I believe. But then you," he said softly, coming closer, "are an old-fashioned girl."

Irene looked up at him, her heart pounding, wondering if he would kiss her, wondering if she would resist.

Instead, he started walking, pulling her past the enormous pool with all the bridges and grottos and foliage and palm trees. He led her up the sweeping steps toward the villa.

Irene felt as if she was a million degrees hot. In spite of her words, she felt as if she wasn't completely in control of herself, not anymore. Not since the moment they'd met. Her rational brain was shouting at her to do something, but the sound was completely obscured by the rush of blood in her own ears, by the pounding of her heart.

She exhaled when he dropped her hand, bending to pick up the beach towels left carelessly on the lounge chairs. He held out her towel. She took it wordlessly, unable to look away as she watched him towel off every inch of his hard, towering, half-naked body.

"So we are what—friends?"

She nearly jumped, and remembered that she, too, should be toweling off. She did it quickly and nodded. "Friends."

"Interesting." A strange gleam was in his dark eyes, illuminated by the lights of the villa. "I've never tried to be friends with a woman."

"No?"

He paused. "Especially one who's driving me out of my mind."

She protested, "I haven't argued anything about your sister's wedding in at least—"

"That's not what I was talking about."

"Oh." She bit her lip, then blurted out, "You can put that aside, right? We can just be friends? Because I need this job. And I can't wonder if, in a moment of weakness, you might…"

"I won't keep you from waiting for your husband," he said softly. "Whoever he may be." He took a deep breath. "But I wonder if there's something you would do for me."

"What?"

Sharif's jaw went hard, and he looked away. It took him several moments to speak, and when he did, his voice was strained.

"I wonder if…after Aziza is wed, and your job

is done…if you'd stay a few extra days. Just until my engagement is announced. Just until—" His voice cut off. He looked at her. "Would you stay with me, Irene, not for money, not as my employee, but just as my friend? Until it's over?"

Beneath his low, rough voice, she heard a hint of isolation, even despair. He was asking for a friend to stand beside him, to wait until the day he was forced to sign his life away. She suddenly realized that being emir, ruler of all but equal of none, must be a strangely lonely experience, in spite of all the servants and palaces and wealth. He was surrounded by people who expected him to be strong. He had to appear powerful at all times. Whom could he ever allow to see any vulnerability or weakness or regret? Who would ever protect *him*?

No one.

If only, Irene thought, *I could be the one to spend my life at his side. We're so different. But maybe we could have been happy just the same.* The thought made a lump rise in her throat. But there was only one thing she could do. She held out her hand.

"Yes, Sharif," she said. "I'll stay till the end."

CHAPTER EIGHT

Sharif stared down through the window of his private office, watching Irene and his sister walk together through the palace garden below.

Irene looked up, as if she felt his gaze. He lifted his hand in greeting. But she abruptly turned away, her sensual body swaying like music as she disappeared with his sister through the garden. He dropped his hand.

Did she know?

Had she guessed?

Grimly, Sharif set his jaw. Every time he saw her, it was harder to hide. He honestly wasn't sure how much longer he could keep it from her.

For three months now, Irene had been living in his palace. For three months, she'd slept in the bedroom across from his. He'd spoken with her, laughed with her. Seen how the rest of the palace staff had come to respect and even love her.

Three months of torture. Of having her join him at dinner, of looking across the table and seeing the sweep of Irene's dark eyelashes trembling against her creamy skin, to see the parting of her full pink lips as she ate and drank and smiled.

Three months of wishing that she, and no other, could be his queen. His *wife*.

Sharif's jaw set as he looked out the window toward the vast sweep of the sparkling gulf. His whole body electrified every time he thought of how it had felt to kiss her in the water that last night in Dubai. He wanted her in his arms. In his bed.

Cold comfort to tell himself that at least no one knew his feelings. He wished he didn't know them himself.

Because Sharif could no longer pretend to himself that what he felt for Irene was lust. He respected her too much for that. It wasn't just friendship, either, no matter how he tried to pretend otherwise. The truth of the matter had hit him hard across the jaw last week, when she'd suddenly burst into laughter at something he'd said—he could no longer even remember what it was—but he'd looked into her sparkling, shining brown eyes, and felt something explode in his chest.

He was in love with her.

In love.

Love wasn't just a myth. It wasn't an illusion. It filled him with light and wonder in a way he'd never felt before. The ache in his heart that expanded until he could think of nothing else. He'd known in that moment that he would do anything for Irene's happiness. Kill for her. Die for her.

He was supposed to be reading through some dry legal documents, in preparation for a phone discussion that afternoon with the Sultan of Zaharqin about a joint oil venture, to be funded both privately and with each nation's sovereign fund. Instead, Sharif had found himself just standing here by the window, on the off chance he might see Irene walking in the garden. And now he had, and now she was gone, his knees were weak and he felt like someone had stabbed his heart with a dagger.

He was in love with Irene.

And he could never have her. Not in marriage. Not without marriage. He couldn't have her in any way.

In one week, his sister would be wed. All he had to do was stay away from Irene for the rest of the week, and he could be done with this torture. He wouldn't have Irene stay another day after that, no matter how he'd once practically begged her. The moment the wedding was done, he would send her away. He'd go back to how he'd felt before.

Numb.

His hand tightened on the window.

"Your Highness, Miss Taylor is asking to see you."

He whirled around to see Hassan, his chief of staff, in the doorway of his office.

"Send her in," he said abruptly, then silently jeered at himself. So much for willpower and staying away from her.

Hassan briefly bowed his head, but as he turned to go, he hesitated, then turned back. "If I might ask your advice, Your Highness...would you think it inappropriate if I were to ask Miss Taylor to accompany me to the party after your sister's wedding—"

"You are forbidden." The hard words came out of Sharif's mouth before he even realized what he was saying. Hassan's eyes widened with shock.

"I see," he said slowly. "Is there some reason that you—"

Sharif tried to be calm. To be cool. But a visceral fury went through him that he could not control and he whirled a fierce, black glare on his trusted friend that would have decimated a lesser man.

Hassan blinked.

"Ah," he said quietly. "So that's the way of it. Does she—"

"No," Sharif said tightly. "She doesn't know and she never will. Once my sister is wed, Miss Taylor will return home. That's the end of it."

"I see." He paused. "The staff love her, sire. Though she was not born in Makhtar, it's clear she loves this country. Your people would joyfully serve her, I think, if you were ever to decide that she—"

"My engagement to Kalila Al-Bahar will be announced next week," Sharif said flatly.

"Oh." Hassan stared at him. He didn't have to say how the palace staff felt about Kalila. After two disastrous visits in the past, Sharif already knew.

"No one must ever know my true feelings for Miss Taylor," he said quietly. "Least of all her. She cannot know. It is bad enough that I do."

"I am sorry," Hassan said. He hesitated. "Shall I still…send her in now?"

Sharif looked at him and shook his head. "It's all over your face." His lip curled. "Go out the back. I will let her in."

Once alone, Sharif took a deep breath. He realized his hands were trembling, so he took a moment to clear the emotion from his heart, from his mind, from his expression. Then he went to open the door.

Irene looked beautiful, he thought, like everything any man could want. She was wearing a simple sheath dress in pale pink, the same color she'd been wearing the moonlit November night they'd met. Her hair was twisted into a thick topknot. Her only makeup was red lipstick. Even her new dark-rimmed glasses made her look, in his current demented state, like a sexy librarian.

"You're wearing glasses," was all he could manage in the way of intelligent conversation.

"I know," she said mournfully. "I lost a contact lens this morning. I've ordered a new pair, but they won't get delivered until later today."

"To what do I owe this pleasure?"

She looked at him, then her expression hardened. "You have to call off this wedding."

How did she know how ardently he'd been wishing that same thing? How had she guessed? In a harsh voice he said, "I cannot. It has been a long-held promise…"

"Not that long," she pointed out, frowning. "Just six months, Aziza said."

Six months? It had been nearly twenty years. It had…

He realized Irene was speaking about his sister's marriage, not his. He'd very nearly blurted out something that would have told her everything. He shook his head, trying to clear the fog from his brain. "Aziza wanted you to speak with me? That's why you rushed away when you saw me at the window?"

"She begged me." Irene's cheeks turned a tantalizing shade of pink. "She felt that…you might listen—to me."

Sharif exhaled. His sister was no fool, though

sometimes she liked to pretend to be one. If she already knew the influence that Irene had over him, how long would it be before everyone knew—including Irene herself?

"We've been through this already," he said.

"She's realized all those gifts you bought her in Dubai are meaningless, compared to throwing her life away! She should be in college, Sharif. She's a bright girl. She should have the chance to—"

"The wedding is in a week. It's too late." Sharif folded his arms, glaring at her. "So if there's nothing else…"

She sighed. "I need to go anyway, or else I'll be late for—"

She bit down hard on her lip.

"Late to where?" he demanded.

Her cheeks had turned a deeper red. "Nothing. Never mind."

Clearly she was hiding something. He had the sudden flash of Hassan's eager face. "Where are you going?"

"I hardly think it matters to—"

"This is my kingdom. You are the chaperone of my sister." Sharif was conscious he was behaving like a brute, but he couldn't stop himself from thundering, "I have full right to know—"

"All right, all right," Irene said irritably. "You don't need to go Total Emir on me. If you must know—" the blush deepened "—I have an appointment for—*hammam.*"

"Hammam?" he repeated in a strangled voice. Against his will, he had the image of Irene totally naked in a steam bath, her body getting slowly rubbed down in the heat, drenched with pails of water, her pink skin invigorated, lightly whipped and wrapped with towels.

"I've heard of nothing else since I came here." She sighed, rolling her eyes. "Apparently it's like having a spa day and a massage and a facial all rolled into one. I promised Aziza I'd go. Since I'll be leaving next week, I'm running out of time."

Her last words hung between them. *Running out of time.* The silence stretched awkwardly, filled with things neither would say.

"Well, I'm off," she said, trying to smile. "Although the thought of getting naked in front of strangers makes me blush."

Naked. Heat pulsed through Sharif's body. All he could think about was how he wished he could be the lucky bath attendant who would touch her, stroke her, caress her naked skin.

He wished he could be free to make love to her.

No. It was more than that.

He wished he could be free to love her.

Turning to go, Irene stopped at the door and looked back at him one last time, her big brown eyes deep and imploring.

"Give Aziza the freedom that you cannot have for yourself, Sharif," she said. "Set her free."

His soul shuddered to the core as he looked at those feverishly bright brown eyes.

"I will think about it," he heard himself say.

Irene blinked in shock. "What?"

He needed her to leave the room, now, before he lost the last thread of his self-control and did something that would ruin someone's life. Possibly many lives. "Just go."

The roughness of his voice made her look sharply at him. She searched his face, then swallowed, stepping back. He wondered what she had seen. Then he knew.

She'd seen the truth on his face, that he was barely holding back from claiming her as his own, against his honor, and damn the consequences.

"I'll go," she stammered, and fled.

Sharif walked around his large polished wood desk. He leaned his arm against the window, then pressed his forehead against the glass. *Give Aziza the freedom that you cannot have for yourself.*

He closed his eyes, remembering when he'd first met his sister. She'd been a tiny, squalling baby placed unsteadily in his teenage arms. She'd been helpless, so small and sad, an unloved orphan. He'd vowed to protect her with his life. He'd vowed he would always love her and take care of her.

You've lived your life for the last nineteen years,

Sharif. He heard his little sister's tearful voice. *What about me? When is my time to live?*

His eyes slowly opened.

He couldn't do it. He was already making the sacrifice of his heart. He couldn't allow his young sister to do the same. She'd made a mistake when she'd agreed to the engagement. But he wouldn't, couldn't, allow her momentary error to become a permanent one.

He would protect her. As he always had.

Turning, he picked up his phone from his desk. He dialed the private number of the Sultan of Zaharqin.

When he reached him, the man was cordial at first, even friendly. But when he realized Sharif wasn't phoning to discuss the potentially huge oil venture, but to cancel the wedding just a few days before the ceremony, the man's voice turned frosty.

"You realize," he said, "that some would consider this affront to be an act of war."

Sharif's body went tight. He had a flash of memory, of his palace burned to ash, of Makhtar City in smoke, of hungry children crying. *No.* But he kept his voice steady. His country had changed. *He* had changed. He was no longer a fifteen-year-old boy. He was now the one in control.

"Makhtar has always been, and always will be, Zaharqin's greatest friend and ally," Sharif said.

"As I am yours. But the hearts of teenagers are changeable. It is regrettable, but there it is. You remember when you were that age…"

"Yes," the sultan said stiffly. "I had already taken my first wife."

"It was a different world, when you and I were young," Sharif said, as if they were the same age.

The man snorted. "You're right about that. Young people today do not know the meaning of duty. Their whims drift on the wind. I should know. My own children—"

The sultan stopped. Sensing weakness, Sharif said smoothly, "Exactly so. But what does not change is friendship, between rulers and between nations. Or the solid profit from good business." He paused. "It would be a pity to let plans for our multi-billion-dollar oil venture falter, merely because of this small personal matter…"

"You really expect me to partner with you? After the mortal insult you've just offered me? I should be calling my generals and telling them to roll our tanks into your city."

"You are free to do so, of course. Free to try. Your generals will warn you about our modern, highly trained army and state-of-the-art defenses. But you could try anyway. Such a mess it would be." He sighed. "A shame to cause the deaths of our most loyal servants and friends, for something so silly as a nineteen-year-old girl deciding she was too young for marriage and motherhood."

"I will be mocked. They'll say the nubile young bride left me at the altar. They'll call me old—me, in my prime! Nothing can compensate for the loss of honor."

"No one will mock you when they hear my sister has left you not for another man, but to study science and literature in college. Your people will say you are well rid of a bride who would have been distracted by academic pursuits from the proper affairs of her high royal position." He paused. "But mostly they will say that you cut me raw, eviscerated my insides from my body, with the deal you made in our oil venture."

"Deal?" The sultan cleared his throat. "What deal?"

It was then that Sharif knew he had him.

"The deal where I take all the financial risk, paying billions of dollars in all the expenses of research, development and transport, and you get all the profit."

After that, it was easy. The man's anger faded, lost in greed and the happy thought of the story that would make the rounds, of how the great Emir of Makhtar had been crushed by his good friend in a business deal. They spoke for some time, hashing out the details of the press release. By the end, the sultan was laughing.

"Even my own children have never cost me so much," he said gleefully. "I wish you joy of her. Please send my best wishes to your sister and thank her, from the bottom of my heart."

Hanging up the phone, Sharif groaned a little, putting his head in his hands. The cost of this little escapade would be far more than any mere shopping spree or diamond trinket. This one would hurt, and he'd be taking it out of his own private fortune. It might take twenty years for his net worth to recover. If it ever did.

But he could live with that. What he couldn't live with was Aziza being unhappy and trapped forever in a loveless marriage. Not his baby sister. Not when he'd vowed to protect her.

But if it wasn't for Irene's interference...

Sharif sucked in his breath. He had to see Irene. Now. He had to tell her that the wedding was off. She had to be the first to know.

Sharif nearly ran down the hall, but Irene's room was empty. Then he remembered. *Hammam.* Turning, he rushed with almost indecorous swiftness to the other side of the palace. The female servants' eyes went wide as he hurried past them, but no one dared to stop the emir as he strode into the dark, quiet, peaceful *hammam* of the women's wing.

He stopped.

It took a moment for his eyes to adjust. He'd never been in here before. The large, hexagon-shaped room was filled with shadows. The high dome soaring overhead was interlaced with patterns of stars, which caused star-shaped beams of sunlight to fall softly into the darkness. Brass lanterns with flickering candles edged the floor, and in the center of the room, a blue pool of water reflected illuminated waves of light on the surrounding dark alcoves.

Only one woman was receiving the pleasures of *hammam*, the steam baths, wraps, massage. Sharif's gaze focused on her.

And he suddenly couldn't breathe.

Irene was lying on a warmed marble slab, facedown with her eyes closed, getting rubbed down by the bath attendant, an older woman who had been hired away from Istanbul long ago. Only a single towel covered Irene's body. As he watched, that towel slipped and fell to the tile floor.

His mouth had already dropped. But seeing Irene naked, his knees shuddered beneath him. He forgot the reason he'd come here. Or maybe suddenly, for the first time, he truly knew it.

The Turkish bath attendant looked at him in surprise, her eyes wide. He held his finger to his lips, then motioned for her to leave.

She looked disapproving, but what could she do? He was the emir. For the first time in his life, Sharif used his raw power for his own selfish purposes.

The woman left, and he took over, pressing his hands against Irene's back, massaging the warm, pink skin of her naked, overheated body.

Aziza had told Irene that the *hammam*, or Turkish bath, would be steamy. "A sort of middle place between heaven and hell," she'd said, then added hastily, "but you'll like it. Trust me."

Irene had already sat naked on a marble slab in a dark alcove for an hour, sweating profusely in steam that was thick as mist. Periodically, the female bath attendant had returned to splash Irene's naked body with hot soapy water, dumped from buckets, then used a coarse hand mitt to scrub her skin from top to bottom. After several times of this procedure, Irene had started to feel like her skin was glowing and also slightly raw.

The worst was that she couldn't see anything in the *hammam* except patterns of shadow and light. She'd taken off her glasses, leaving them with her clothes in the changing room. Without them, she felt disoriented, even helpless, but maybe it was all for the best. Getting totally naked in front of a stranger, even one as businesslike as the female attendant, was a brand-new experience. Without glasses, and with no contact lenses either, she couldn't tell if the attendant was judging the shape of her body. Irene couldn't have even said what the attendant's face looked like. Especially in the deep shadows of the *hammam*. The only light came from the enormous dome above, gleaming tiny pinpoints of light, leaving dappled stars onto the white marble. Heaven and hell indeed.

Just like the last three months had been.

She'd seen Sharif every day, lived in the same palace, even the same hallway. Every morning, every evening, she'd sat across from him at the dining table. She'd seen his darkly handsome face, heard his voice. They'd spoken about politics and world affairs; they'd discussed Makhtar's recent international film festival and new art gallery. And that was just in public. In private, when they were alone, they'd teased each other about everything and nothing.

Sharif knew her now. He knew her as no one ever had. He knew her, though he hadn't kissed her since that night in Dubai.

After she'd started learning Arabic with a Makhtari tutor, Sharif had asked her to be his de facto hostess, entertaining ambassadors and heads of state. Breathlessly, Irene had dressed in designer gowns from local boutiques. She'd entered the ballroom on his arm. Once she would have been shy and afraid of strangers, but now, at his side, she was ready to do battle, to do her best to charm his friends and enemies alike. For him. All for him.

She wanted to make him proud. She wanted

to make his dark eyes gleam as he smiled at her across the ballroom. And afterward, when they were alone, she wanted to hear him say in his deep, sensual voice, "Thank you, Miss Taylor. You are a pearl beyond measure. Makhtar is grateful for your service."

"I know," she would tease in reply. "You're seriously lucky to have me. All the other emirs keep calling."

He would laugh, then his eyes would turn dark and he would start to say something—then stop himself. Irene would catch her breath and turn away. Without even asking what he could not say. Because she knew.

Heaven had turned to hell. Having Sharif so close, but never being able to touch him, never being able to say what was truly in her heart…it was agony.

How could she bear to stay another day?

How could she ever bear to go?

In a week, whether she was willing or no, Irene would leave Makhtar forever. Aziza would be married to a man three times her age, and Sharif would take as his queen a woman he despised. No one was marrying for love here. All those lives ruined.

Including, she was starting to fear, her own.

"Stop thinking," the bath attendant barked in English, sloughing Irene's shoulders with the rough hand mitt, scrubbing her skin until she flinched. "Too tense!"

"Yes." She sighed, and tried to obey. The woman pulled her to standing and rinsed her with a shock of cold water, then stepped back and made some sort of gesture. She waited expectantly.

"I'm sorry, I can't see," Irene said apologetically for the tenth time.

"Come," the woman said roughly in English, grabbing her hand. "I take."

She led Irene out of the alcove, to the center of the *hammam*, beneath the dome. She gently pushed her to lie down, with her naked belly against the marble slab in the center of the room, on the edge of the illuminated blue pool. Irene sighed as she felt the cool marble beneath her skin. Her backside was covered with a towel, and thick white steam floated beneath the tiny beams of light, between the shadows.

"Close eyes," the attendant said, and Irene obeyed. She tried not to think, not to let herself feel the rising heartbreak inside her, but quiet her mind and soul and just let the attendant's hands massage the aching muscles of her shoulders.

But just as Irene started to relax, the hands were gone. She heard a heavy step, the attendant's intake of breath. Then the hands returned to rubbing her back, even more intently than before.

She tried not to think about Sharif. It was impossible. In just a week, Irene would leave this country, and never see him again... Never feel his eyes on hers. Never feel the heat of his body as he brushed innocently against her in the hallway. Never feel his hand take hers, or the soft innocent press of his lips against her cheek. Never see his smile, or the wicked gleam of his dark eyes.

Cold water was splashed on her naked body in the semidarkness. She heard the hiss of hot coals. Felt the hard, firm hands slowly kneading into her tense back, going slower, deeper...

Why couldn't she forget Sharif? Why wasn't this working?

She couldn't be falling in love with him. She *couldn't*. He was promised to another. And she'd made promises to herself, to her own future, that she intended to keep.

How she wished there had been another choice. But there wasn't. Soon, another woman—his bride and queen—would take Irene's place at all those diplomatic dinners.

"Walk with me," Sharif had said quietly last night, as he often did when they were dining just as a family, without all the fuss and pomp of ceremony. For two hours after dinner, they'd been alone, walking together in the moonlight of the garden. But for the first time, there had been no teasing laughter between them. No laughter of any kind.

"What is the emir's future bride like?" she'd asked Basimah wistfully that morning.

The older woman had turned red. "Do not ask me about her."

"But you've met her. Aziza said your sister worked in her household once, was even her personal maid."

"The emir is getting what he deserves, that's all I'll say," Basimah muttered. "Making my poor lamb marry that sultan. If I could do something to prevent his wedding, if I knew something that would prevent it, I still wouldn't lift a finger. That's all I'm going to say about his fine bride with her fine fancy feathers. They deserve each other."

So Irene had been forced to go looking online for pictures of the Makhtari heiress. It didn't make her feel better. The beautiful future queen of Makhtar was all brilliant eyes and severe cheekbones and pouting red lips, skinny as a rail and always dressed in the highest fashion.

She'd seen pictures of Kalila Al-Bahar at a royal polo match... Skiing in Gstaad... Coming out of a club in London, dressed in a fur... Attending a royal wedding. After graduating from an expensive boarding school in Switzerland, she had skipped college to become a full-time jet-setter. She would fit into Sharif's world as she, Irene, never could.

The pressure gentled on her back. Rough fingertips slid down her naked skin in a way that was distinctively…sensual. And Irene's eyes flew open.

Twisting her head, she looked back and saw a dark blur. She couldn't see a face. But she knew.

"What are you doing here?" she choked out. "You aren't supposed to be in here!"

Sharif's voice was low, even silky. "I rule this country. I can go where I please."

"Not in the women's bath in the palace!" Sitting up, she tried to twist around in a way that would hide her body. It was impossible. She wanted to cover herself with a towel, but couldn't find it. She was naked, sitting on a slab of marble, in the hot steam of the *hammam*, alone with the man she wanted most. The man she couldn't—mustn't—have!

"What are you doing here?" she cried again, covering her breasts with her arms.

She felt, rather than saw, his eyes slowly rake over her body.

"I came to…" His voice was hoarse. "To tell you…"

His words trailed off. He abruptly pulled her against him.

"Irene," he whispered against her lips. She felt his hands grip her upper arms. Felt the heat of the steam room and the rawness of her pink, freshly scrubbed skin. His hands tightened. She heard his ragged intake of breath.

And he savagely lowered his mouth to hers.

This kiss had nothing of tenderness in it. It was searing. Hungry. Demanding. It took possession, hard and deep.

She felt Sharif's lips on hers, and after her three months of yearning, something snapped inside her. She forgot she was naked—or didn't care—she just needed him, needed this, or she would die. Wrapping her arms around him, she returned the kiss desperately, kissing him back so hard that it bruised her lips, needing to taste him, to possess him in return.

He shoved her back against the marble, kissing her as if he'd lost his mind, and she kissed him back with equal force, because she'd certainly lost hers. They held each other in a frenzy of mutual passion and need. He roughly started pulling off his clothes, ripping off his shirt, then his trousers. Above the hiss of water dripping against hot coals on the other side of the darkened, domed room, empty of everything except the six-sided marble slab surrounding the illuminated blue water of the pool and the pinpoints of light above, she heard the gasp of his breath as he pulled her back hungrily into his arms. His hands swept down her naked skin, and she touched him all over, realizing he was naked, too. Naked against her, in the hot, steamy *hammam*, suspended directly between heaven and hell.

She kissed him, nibbling on his lower lip, gasping as she felt his hands cup her aching breasts. He licked up her neck, sucked on the tender flesh of her earlobe, then moved down her body, tasting every inch of her as he went down, down to the valley between her breasts.

"I've wanted you—for so long," he choked out. "For months I've thought only of you—"

He pushed her full breasts together with his large hands, pressing his lips in the cleavage between before he moved to suckle her. She cried out. She'd never felt any sensation like this before. Never imagined what it could be.

She twisted on the marble as he moved down her body, his wet, hard body sliding slowly against hers. He gripped her hips, then went down farther. She trembled beneath him as his fingertips traced the outside edge of her body, her waist to hips to knees, all the way to the sensitive soles of her feet, which he kissed, one by one. Then he slowly moved upward, pushing her legs apart—kissing to her inner knees—upward, upward…

He used his powerful hands to part her thighs. He lowered his head. Irene suddenly couldn't breathe, as she felt the warmth and heat of his breath against her most sensitive core. If some part of her was screaming that she had to stop, stop this now, she wouldn't let herself hear it. Later. She'd let herself think later. When her body wasn't on fire with need for him… For only him….

He inhaled, exhaled, as if breathing her into the rhythm of his own heart. Then he moved his head closer and licked her inside thigh. Her eyes squeezed shut, her lips parted in a gasp. He moved up higher, gripping her legs, holding her down against the marble. Finally, with agonizing slowness, he lowered his head.

He took a long, lingering taste between her legs, so deep and slow that her hips bucked with the intense wave of pleasure that crashed over her, nearly drowning her with desire and need.

"Sharif…" she gasped. "You…you can't…"

But he could. And he did. Using his mouth and tongue, he teased her, using her body as if he'd known it all his life. As if he knew it better than she did. She twisted beneath him, side to side, nearly weeping with the weight of her desire. She would do anything. Anything.

As he continued to lick and suckle her aching wet core, she felt him push a single thick fingertip inside her. Then another. He invaded her tight, virgin body, slowly stretching her with his fingertips, as she expanded to accept him inside her. Caught in the onslaught of brutal pleasure she'd never imagined possible, her body went tighter and tighter still, as her hips lifted of their own accord. Her lips parted with a long intake of breath that seemed to go on and on and on, until she felt dizzy beneath the shadows and light of the Turkish bath, beneath Sharif himself, as the world spun around her, and sent her flying.

She hung on to his shoulders with her fingernails as she flew and flew. She heard a scream as the black-and-white world exploded into a million bright colors, and fell, chiming like music.

Sharif moved over her almost instantly, lifting his body so that the thick hardness of him was between her legs, demanding entry.

She lay beneath him, limp with pleasure, unable to resist. *Not wanting* to resist. Any thoughts she'd once had of the future or honor were washed away from her mind, like sand beneath an ocean wave. Who cared about something so unimportant as the future? What was that, compared to this?

He drew back his hips, to plunge inside her.

Her eyes lifted to his face. Even this close, she couldn't see his face. All she could see was shadow.

The moment before he would have entered her, he hesitated. He held himself still.

Then, with a low curse, he rolled off her.

It took several moments before she realized he wasn't coming back. She blinked, struggling to understand, to awaken from the sensual haze.

Something white flew toward her. Looking

down at her lap, she saw a towel. He'd thrown her a towel?

"Get dressed," he growled. Bending over the tile floor, he picked up his trousers and pulled them over his naked, hard, unsatisfied body.

Irene's throat suddenly hurt. She looked down at the towel, at her own naked body. She'd thrown herself at him, she realized. She'd been willing to throw everything away for the sake of a single moment—and *he was turning her down*.

"I don't understand," she said in a small voice.

"Don't you?" he said in low fury.

Wrapping herself in the towel, she rose from the marble. She felt humiliated. *She hadn't known.* She hadn't fully realized how overwhelming sex could be, the need that could block out all reason, as primal as the need to breathe or eat or sleep.

Close as she was, without her glasses, she still couldn't see his face. As her cheeks turned hot in shame, she was glad. "I can't imagine what you think of me."

"No. You can't."

She said over the razor blade in her throat, "Was it to teach me a lesson? That I'm nothing more than a naive fool, a prude, with my ridiculous dreams of love and saving myself—"

"No," he cut her off. "It wasn't a lesson." She saw the tension of his shoulders, the set of his body that was like a trap waiting to snap shut. "It was a mistake."

"I never knew it could feel like that." She suddenly felt like crying. "I'm sorry."

"*You're* sorry?" Going to her, he lifted her chin, forcing her to meet his gaze. Now they were so close, she finally saw his agonized dark eyes. "I am to blame," he ground out. "Only me. When I came here, I never meant…but I saw you and—" Dropping his hand, he clawed back his dark hair. "I am the only one to blame."

So it hadn't been a test? Her heart started beating again. "Then why did you stop? I couldn't have stopped you."

"You could have stopped me at any time—just by saying no."

"But I couldn't. The way it felt…" Irene took a shuddering breath. "I lost all control, I lost my mind. If it wasn't a test, then I don't understand. You had me in your power. Why didn't you…"

"Why didn't I take you?"

Wordlessly, she nodded.

Sharif stared at her for a long moment. "You say that you now understand how overwhelming passion can be. I now understand what you were talking about as well. Making love should be an expression of love. Love that lasts forever." Reaching out, he stroked her cheek and whispered, "I won't take your dream away from you."

Irene realized that tears were spilling over her lashes. And it was in this moment that she knew, knew it to her very blood and bones, that if she'd made love with him today it would have only been the expression of what was in her heart.

She loved him. All of him, his honor and ferocity and humor and selfishness, all of him, with every bit of her soul.

"Sharif..." she choked out. *Don't marry that other woman, beautiful as she is. Marry me. Love me.*

"You're getting what you want," he said in a low voice. "That's what I came to tell you."

She gaped at him.

He gave her a smile that didn't meet his eyes. Dropping his hand, he stepped back. "I've canceled my sister's wedding, Miss Taylor. You've won."

"Aziza's free?" Irene closed her eyes as she pictured the young girl's face. She looked at him in gratitude. "Thank you."

"No. Thank you. For reminding me of my place."

"But what about you?"

His expression hardened. His voice was even as he said, "Canceling Aziza's wedding means that my own must go forward as soon as possible. I will be phoning Kalila and—"

"I saw pictures of her," Irene said miserably. "She's beautiful."

"Yes," he said dully. He exhaled with a flare of nostril, looking away. "Very beautiful."

Looking at him, Irene's heart broke.

"Don't do it," she said. "Don't marry her."

"I gave my word."

"Break it," she said desperately.

He gave a low, humorless laugh. "You are saying this? *You*?"

She swallowed, remembering all the times she'd insisted on honor, on love, on the importance of marriage and honesty.

He looked at her. "Even if I could discard my honor so lightly, Kalila comes from a powerful Makhtari family. If I offended her father, it would start trouble. It could even start a war."

"It's not fair," she said tearfully. "You made the promise when you were fifteen—a boy!"

"I knew what I was doing." He pushed back a tendril of her damp hair. "And if I could so lightly break my promise to Kalila, how could anyone ever trust my word again?" Looking down at her, he said softly, "How could you?"

"I could," Irene insisted, even if part of her wondered. She gripped the towel wrapped tightly over her breasts, over her breaking heart. "I know you, Sharif," she said, her voice cracking. "Honor, caring for your family, for your country—that's everything to you. You can't—"

A heavy door banged against the wall. Cold air rushed into the *hammam*, causing the steam to melt away. Irene jumped when she saw the bath attendant rush in. The woman didn't even look at her, just went straight to Sharif and spoke in rapid Arabic. The words were too quick for Irene to understand, but she saw the instant tension of Sharif's body, like a man who'd just been cut with steel.

"What is it?" she asked as the attendant bowed and hurried away. "What's happened?"

Sharif walked to a wall. He flicked on an electric switch, and the bath was suddenly filled with harsh light, causing all the shadows and mysteries to disappear, leaving only cold reality.

"You need to get dressed." His voice had no expression.

Something was wrong. Something was very wrong. Longing to put her arms around his naked chest, to offer him comfort, she went close to him, trying to see his face. He looked at her. He was once again the powerful emir in control. The vulnerable man she'd so briefly seen beneath the mask had disappeared as if he'd never been.

Emotionlessly Sharif said, "My future bride has seen fit to honor us with a visit."

Irene's lips parted. "You can't mean—"

"Kalila has just arrived unexpectedly at the palace." He turned empty eyes to hers. "Come, Miss Taylor," he said. "Come meet my beautiful bride."

CHAPTER NINE

"You can't trust servants. Any of them." Kalila Al-Bahar's red-nailed hand waved airily over the dining room table. "Thieves and liars, most of them. And the precious few who aren't, well, they're generally stupid and lazy."

Irene blushed, exchanging glances with Aziza, who sat wide-eyed beside her. Kalila seemed completely unaware that the long dinner table was, in fact, surrounded by twelve palace servants, all of them within earshot, all of them stone-faced.

"Oh," Kalila turned to Irene with a saccharine-sweet smile on her sharp red lips, "I do beg your pardon. Of course I didn't mean *you*, Miss Taylor. I'm sure you're…none of these things."

"Of course," Irene said through gritted teeth. Her eyes met Sharif's. He was at the head of the table, in his traditional white robes, as was right and proper for the Emir of Makhtar entertaining the daughter of the former vizier, now wealthy governor of Makhtar's eastern region.

Sharif's handsome face was as expressionless as a statue, but oh, she knew what he was feeling. Her heart twisted painfully.

This horrible woman was to be his wife—the partner of his life—the mother of his children?

Irene had been so nervous to meet the beautiful Kalila. After leaving Sharif at the *hammam*, she'd rushed to her room, tidied up, showered and dressed. She'd been relieved to see a new box of contact lenses from the local optometrist waiting on her writing desk. Her hands had trembled as she put on red lipstick and a simple black sheath dress, adding a rope of fake pearls around her neck, like armor.

As if any lipstick or fake pearls could make Irene compete with Kalila Al-Bahar. When Irene had first met her at the start of dinner, she'd been overwhelmed with misery. The Makhtari heiress was even more beautiful and thin and impossibly glamorous in person. She had dark eyes lined with kohl, dark hair streaked blond, red lips, long red fingernails, tight red dress. The February weather in Makhtar was pleasantly warm, but she'd still draped herself in a mink coat. She looked like a gorgeous 1950s film star, Irene had thought, crossed with a dash of anorexic porn actress.

Then Kalila had started to speak, and she hadn't stopped since. She had a beautiful, husky, magical voice. But she dominated every conversation with selfish, ugly words.

"If I had my way," she continued now, "I'd bury every servant in the desert, and replace them with—I don't know, anything. Trained dogs. Robots." She sighed. "But robot technology is just so damn slow."

The silence that greeted this bombshell was immediate. Even Kalila sensed something in the air.

"But enough about that." She turned abruptly to Aziza. "I heard you like to shop. I should take you shopping."

"Thank you," Aziza murmured, tossing Irene a panicked look out of the corner of her eye.

"Do not worry," Kalila said kindly. "I can show you where to go and what to buy. Once you are in my hands, in the right clothes, we'll be able to disguise how you're so hideously fat and plain."

Aziza gave a funny little intake of breath.

Irene saw the pain in the younger girl's face, and her lips parted as if she'd taken the blow herself. It was one thing to insult *her*—Irene could take it—but to purposefully hurt someone as sweet and defenseless as Aziza…

Putting her hands on the table, Irene started to rise to her feet, intending to say something sharp and reckless. But Sharif beat her to it.

"Enough, Kalila." He was standing at the end of the table, cold fury on his face. "You will apologize to my sister for your words that are both hateful and untrue."

Glaring at him, Kalila tossed her head. "High time someone told the girl to do something with herself!"

"It's all right, brother." Aziza tried to smile, but her eyes still looked suspiciously moist. "She's right. I have many flaws. I could stand to lose a few pounds." She looked down at her tightly folded hands, all her usual excitement deflated as she whispered, "I am lucky that the sultan even wants to marry me..."

Sharif stared at her.

"No," he said gently. "I meant to tell you. You won't be marrying him, after all."

Her eyes widened, then she said miserably, "Did he change his mind because I'm too fat?"

Her confidence was so shot, Irene wished ardently to slap the cold superior smile off Kalila's face.

"*No*. He wanted to marry you. But I called it off," Sharif said firmly. He glanced at Irene. "Miss Taylor convinced me that college is the proper place for a young woman as bright and determined as you."

"Bright?" Aziza breathed. "Determined?"

Walking to her place at the table, Sharif put his hand on his young half sister's shoulder. "Yes," he said quietly. "And brave and strong. Your whole life is ahead of you. You might become a scientist, an economist, who knows? There are many ways for a princess to benefit her country." He smiled down at her. "You will do good things for Makhtar in ways I cannot even yet dream. I trust you to find the right path."

"Oh, brother…" Bursting into tears, Aziza rose to her feet and threw her arms around him. "Thank you," she breathed. She shook her head, wiping her eyes. "You won't regret this."

Watching them, Irene had a lump in her throat.

"You're throwing away her only chance for a good marriage," Kalila said, looking down at her red-tipped nails. "No man will ever want to marry a fat, smart girl."

It was the final straw. Throwing her hands against the table, Irene jumped to her feet. "You horrible, dreadful woman!" she cried. "You, be queen of Makhtar? You're not fit to even clean the palace bathrooms!"

Kalila looked at her, all cold, thin, glamorous beauty.

"Ah, so the claws come out at last," she murmured, "of the famous Miss Taylor that half this city has fallen in love with." She narrowed her eyes, and Irene suddenly wondered if she'd heard rumors—if she was the reason that Kalila had come here so abruptly. Tilting her head, the heiress said with venomous sweetness, "But with

Aziza's wedding canceled and her leaving for college soon, there is no reason for you to remain here anymore as her companion, is there? I will thank you to leave my table."

Irene shook with rage. "*Your* table?"

"Yes. My table," she said coldly. She waved her skeletal arm. "This palace will be mine. The country will be mine." With a hard smile, she looked straight into Irene's eyes. "Sharif will be mine."

Kalila's vicious words sliced through Irene's heart, causing her to stagger back.

The other woman watched her reaction with spiteful pleasure, then turned to Sharif and said sweetly, "I have finally decided to set a date. With your sister's engagement off, we will officially announce our engagement tonight."

"No…" The word was a barely audible whisper, coming unbidden from Irene's heart.

Sharif stood beside his sister, his shoulders tight, as cold and expressionless as a statue.

"Well?" Kalila said.

He glanced at Irene. For an instant, she saw the flash of pain in his dark eyes. Then he turned to Kalila with perfect manners and no emotion whatsoever.

"As you wish. It will be arranged within the hour."

"And since all our country is expecting a royal

wedding at the end of the week…" She waved her arm, causing her diamond and platinum bangles to clink together loudly. "It would be a waste of money not to take advantage of the arrangements already in place, don't you think?"

A dawning horror rose in Irene's heart.

Sharif's expression sharpened. "We cannot simply switch my sister's wedding for ours, Kalila. Royal protocol must be followed."

"*You* are emir. *You* set the protocol." Kalila tilted her head. "Unless you have changed your mind. Surely you do not wish to disappoint our people, Sharif? Surely—" her voice took an edge "—you do not wish to insult my father?"

Brief hatred flared in his eyes, then died.

"No," he said dully. "I do not."

Irene grabbed his arm desperately. "Sharif," she gasped, too stricken to realize she was calling him by his first name in front of everyone in the dining room, "Please. You cannot…"

He looked down at her.

"My bride is right," he said coldly. "We no longer need you, Miss Taylor."

"What?" Irene whispered, dropping her hand. He was staring at her as if she were a stranger. As if they hadn't spent all these months together. As if, just a few hours before, he hadn't nearly made love to her. As if she were nothing and no one.

She swallowed, blinking fast. She shook her head.

"But I can't..." she choked out. *I can't leave you.* Then she looked around the dining hall, at Kalila staring at her smugly, at Aziza with big eyes in her pale face, at the servants who were trying and failing to pretend they weren't hearing every word.

Turning away from them, Irene looked at the handsome face of the man she loved.

"But I love you," she whispered.

Sharif seemed to flinch, as if he'd taken a bullet to the heart. But his expression was granite as he looked at her.

"Thank you for your service," he said, making the words meaningless and cold. "You will be paid the entire amount, as agreed." When she did not move, his jaw hardened. He grabbed her wrist. "It is time for you to leave."

Without another word, he physically pulled her from the cavernous dining hall. Once in the hallway, he dragged her hard along with him, speaking sharply in Arabic to his bodyguards as they passed. The bodyguards fell into place behind him, one of them speaking into his earpiece to someone else unseen. Irene looked at Sharif's face. "What are you doing?"

He looked at her. "I'm sending you away. To the future you deserve."

Irene wondered how she could have not known immediately, beneath the pretense of the playboy she'd first seen in Italy, exactly who he was. A good-hearted man. She should have loved him from the moment he'd first pursued her on the shores of Lake Como. Fighting back tears, she shook her head. "I won't leave you."

He looked away, tightening his grip on her arm, pulling her rapidly down the long hallways of the palace. "You must."

"Not like this," she choked out. "Not with *her*."

Sharif stopped, his face grim. He signaled to his bodyguards, and they moved ahead without him. Once alone, he cupped her cheek, looking at her urgently.

"Kalila will be my wife. I've always known this. From the very day I met you, Irene, at the wedding of someone I barely knew, I was trying to accept my fate. I couldn't then. But—" he took a deep breath "—I can now."

"What?" she said, stricken.

He looked down. "Because of you," he said in a low voice. "Because of what you taught me."

"I never taught you to marry someone you hate, someone who is horrible like that—to make her the queen of your country—"

"You taught me how to believe again." He looked up. "You taught me to love. For the rest of my life. As I will love you."

Their eyes locked in the shadows.

Then a sob escaped her as she flung her arms around him, pressing her cheek against his chest, against his white robes. "I can't leave you. I won't. It's too soon—"

Fervently, he kissed her forehead, her hair. "Better now than later. Before anything happens that we both—regret."

Tears were running openly down her face. "I regret only that I didn't let you make love to me every single day." Looking up at him, she shook her head. "I should have let you kiss me, from the night we first met—"

"Shh." He put his finger on her lips. "It is better this way. You'll find someone who can make you happy. Who can give you what I never could."

"Another man?" The thought was like death. "How can you even hope that for me?"

His black eyes looked infinitely deep and sad. "Because I need your happiness more than my own."

A bodyguard came back and gave him a nod. Sharif turned back to her and said simply, "It is time."

Gently taking her hand in his own, he pulled her out a side door and into the warm night. She heard the burble of the fountain, the soft cry of night birds. She saw the black outline of palm trees swaying against a violet sky scattered with stars. She loved everything about this country. Somehow, it had become home to her. Every part of it—especially its emir...

Then she saw a limousine waiting to take her to the airport.

"No!" she cried, backing up desperately. She tried to think of an excuse to linger, just ten minutes more. Five. "My clothes—I need to pack my things…"

"It will be arranged. Here is your bag. Your passport." He snapped his fingers and a bodyguard gave him something. Sharif held out her purse. "My plane is waiting to take you home. Your final paycheck will be transferred to your bank account in Colorado before you land."

This was really happening. "How can you do this to me?"

"Do it to you?" He took a deep breath. "It's *for* you that I'm doing this."

"At least let me stay the week. I will stay here with you until the bitter end. Even—" she lifted her gaze to his "—after…"

His lips parted with shock. "You mean, even after I am wed, you would—"

Her voice was small. "I won't leave you. Not even then."

Sharif stared at her, then shook his head fiercely. "*No.* Even if you were willing to give up all your dreams, I wouldn't let you." Pulling her into his arms, he searched her gaze. "Don't you understand? I have to believe in something.

Something more than just cold duty to my country. And it's you."

Her legs were trembling. She clung to his shoulders, barely holding on. She wanted to fall to her knees and wrap her arms around him and beg him not to make her leave, at any cost.

"Don't marry her. Marrying someone you hate will ruin your life."

"It is already ruined," he said softly, looking at her, and suddenly tears were choking her as she read everything in his eyes.

"Sharif—"

"I love you, Irene," he said. "For the first time in my life, I understand what that means. Because my love for you will last for the rest of my life." He cupped her cheek. "You were right."

A sob escaped her. "No—"

"Be happy," he whispered. He kissed her one last time with all his passion, his lips tender and yearning and full of grief and love. Then he let her go. He held up his hand, and two bodyguards came forward to escort her into the limo.

"Sharif," she screamed, fighting them. "Sharif!"

But they pushed her into the backseat of the car, and the door was slammed shut behind her. As the limo sped away, Irene looked back with a sob through the rear window. She saw Sharif's forlorn figure get smaller and smaller in front of the palace, until he disappeared altogether and all she had left of him was that last image of his stricken face, burned forever into her heart.

Long after the limo had disappeared past the palace gate, Sharif remained immobile, staring at the clouds of dust on the road. He closed his eyes, still seeing Irene's tear-stained face as it had looked through the rear window. He knew he'd never see her again.

"Your Highness?"

He opened his eyes bleakly to see Hassan standing in the side door of the palace. "I have the head of the top Makhtar PR agency on the phone," he said. "He's saying he received an urgent message. I can of course take a message if you—"

"No," Sharif said, and barely recognized his own voice. Kalila must have called them immediately—but then, she knew all the angles. She'd probably already announced their engagement on her social media accounts, making it all sound romantic, making everyone envious of their *great love*. "Ask him to come to the palace at once. We're going to announce our engagement."

"You and Miss—"

"To Kalila," he cut him off.

"But—Miss Taylor?"

"I sent her home."

"But you...I thought..." He hesitated. "When the rumor swept through that you'd rushed to see her in the women's *hammam*, the whole staff greatly hoped..."

"Speak to me no more of Miss Taylor," he said harshly. He turned away. "Let's get this over with."

"Get what over with, exactly, Your Highness?"

"My engagement. My wedding." *My life*.

After they returned to the palace, his chief of staff and bodyguards went their separate ways, as each man's duty required. And so did Sharif.

He walked slowly down the hallway, back toward the dining room. But with every step farther away from Irene, the strength seemed to leave his body. He felt like an old man. No. He felt as if he'd already died.

He stopped.

Irene. Her name was like a prayer in his heart. He pressed his fists hard against his eyes. She would have everything he could not give her. A man who would love her, marry her, have children with her. All her dreams would come true, even without him. He had to believe he'd done the right thing. Loving her, remembering the brief moments they'd shared, would have to be enough to sustain him for the rest of his life. The memory of her, and the knowledge that she'd someday be happy with someone else...

Bleakly, he went back to the dining room. It was empty. His sister had left. His servants had cleared the table.

Only one person remained, standing by the open window, smoking a cigarette. She turned to face him.

"So you tossed her out," Kalila said. "I confess you surprised me. I did not expect you to let this one go so easily."

"What do you want, Kalila?" he said wearily.

She gave him a hard smile. "Your assurance that, after we are wed and I give you your heir, you will leave me alone, with all the same rights to play that you have."

Sharif stared at his future bride in the shadows of the empty dining hall. "We are not yet wed, and you are planning how you wish to be unfaithful?"

She gave a cold laugh. "Don't take that outraged tone with me. I'm not one of your doe-eyed little virgins." She took another elegant drag off her cigarette. "Not like *her*."

He jolted. "You knew we were never lovers?"

"Of course, I could tell. Stupid little virgin, hanging on your every word, staring up at you with those big needy eyes." She took another puff. Her fingers were almost as thin and white as the cigarette. "Have her, if you want. And I intend to have my own fun. I don't care if you hate me. Our marriage is about power, not *love*."

She made the word a sneer. Just as he once had.

"When you are my queen," Sharif said tightly,

"I expect you to rule with respect and dignity for our customs and laws."

She shrugged her skinny shoulders. "I'm no fool. I'll be discreet."

"This I doubt."

She snorted. "More than you have been," she said pointedly, "sneaking around with your sister's companion. Even if you weren't lovers, I heard whispers about your—*relationship*—all the way to New York. My father was the one who called me."

Sharif's lips twisted sardonically. "So that is why you raced here? Because you feared I wouldn't keep my word—that I would marry her?"

Kalila looked away abruptly, then lifted the cigarette to her lips with trembling fingers. "I should have nailed this down a long time ago." Looking out the window, she said in a low voice, "I won't let one mistake keep me from everything that should be mine."

Sharif's eyes narrowed. "She wasn't a mistake."

"What? Oh. Yes. Miss Taylor. But she's gone now. And we understand each other, do we not?" She jerked her chin with glittering eyes. "We'll be wed next week in your sister's place. Then we will consummate the marriage…as often and frequently as we must…"

He tried not to flinch.

"Once you get me pregnant, I do not care what

you do. Bring your precious Miss Taylor back. Install her in your bed, for all I care." Kalila abruptly put out her cigarette on the windowsill, leaving a burn mark before she dropped the cigarette carelessly to the floor. He watched the lingering ashes fall against his tile floor like gray snowflakes. "It means nothing to me."

Staring at her, Sharif had a sudden flashback to shining brown eyes. *When I marry, it will only be for love. And our wedding night will be truly about making love. The kind that will last forever.* He remembered the tremble of Irene's voice just an hour before, when she'd told him she loved him.

"Our marriage is nothing but a means to an end," Kalila said. "Something to endure, and ignore, until we both are dead."

He abruptly focused on her face, on those black eyes with fake black lashes, beautiful, yes, but so cold, with an almost reptilian stare. So different from loving, warm brown eyes that glowed at you with the heat of summer, like the warmth of an embrace. He looked at his fiancée's hollow cheekbones, so different from the healthy rose-dusted cheeks that blushed with modesty or shyness or even anger.

Kalila didn't seem to feel anything, care about anything, so long as she had two things: money and power. She wanted the prestige of being Her Highness, the Sheikha of Makhtar, the mother of the future heir—and the pleasure of enjoying herself with any man she pleased during the length of their marriage.

She was shallow. Terminally shallow.

And once, Sharif suddenly realized, he'd been just like her. Oh, he'd always cared about doing his duty by his country, and by his family. But other than that, he'd cared for nothing and no one. He'd wasted endless days on meaningless love affairs, trying to distract himself from his own empty soul.

Then he'd had the grace and fortune to meet Irene. It was the miracle of his life.

And the tragedy.

"Not a word in reply?" Kalila took a step toward him, frowning. "What has changed in you, Sharif?"

"What are you talking about?"

"You're different somehow. You…" She sucked in her breath, covering her hand over her mouth with an astonished giggle. "But wait. Don't tell me you're actually in love with her?"

"Be quiet," he snapped.

"Your sweet virgin. So tender. So true…"

"She's worth a thousand of you," he said.

"You love her." Kalila cackled a laugh. "The great Emir of Makhtar is chained down at last. How very amusing to see you caught this way. Just like—"

"Like what?" he said, expecting an insult. She looked away.

"Nothing," she muttered. "It's just funny, that's all. Your precious Miss Taylor—"

He grabbed her wrist.

"Don't ever," he said in a low, dangerous voice, "speak her name again."

Kalila blinked, then gave another low laugh. "Have it your way." She ripped her bony arm from his grasp. "Keep your sweet memories. I will take my throne." Her eyes were feverishly bright. "I think this marriage will suit me very well."

CHAPTER TEN

FIVE DAYS LATER, Irene was in Colorado, kneeling on the ramshackle porch of her old house, boxing up the last items to take north to their new place in Denver. There was surprisingly little to pack. Some of her family's old possessions, worn clothes like her mother's pink terry hot pants with the word *Tasty* emblazoned across the backside, had gone straight into the trash. A few other things had gone to the local charity shop. But her sister and her mother had already taken the things they cared about when they'd left here four days ago.

Her sister, Melissa, was already unpacking boxes in the brand-new condo in Denver that Irene had leased, right between the local community college and Colorado's best private rehab facility, where their mother had checked herself in two days ago. Melissa was studying to take her GED test, to compensate for never having graduated from high school, and looking eagerly through the college course book. A rough road might still lie ahead, Irene knew, but it was going to work out. They were going to be settled and secure, and have the chance to be happy.

"Thank you, baby," her mother had said, openly weeping when she hugged Irene close, the last moment before she went into rehab. "I wanted to be a good mother to you. I tried. But I didn't know how." She wiped her eyes hard. "I'm going to learn."

Melissa had cried, too—when she first saw the luxury condo on a lovely, tree-lined street in Denver, and the college book sitting on the kitchen counter. "You remembered how I used to talk about becoming a dental assistant?"

Irene nodded.

"Do you know how much they make per hour?" Melissa demanded, then she, too, wiped her eyes. "Plus, they hang around with handsome single dentists all day…"

"You'd be a great assistant. Or you could be a dentist yourself."

"Me?"

"Sure." Irene had shrugged. "Let all the sexy male dental assistants come to you."

"You think I could?" her sister had breathed as if considering the idea for the first time. "And you'd pay for me to go to dental school?"

"Any kind of school you want." Irene had

reached out and taken her sister's hand. "I believe in you."

Melissa blinked back tears. "I always thought you judged me…"

"I did," Irene said. "I did and I'm sorry. I didn't understand then how powerful sex and love can be. Or that sometimes, no matter how hard you try—" she looked down "—dreams don't always come true…"

"Dreams don't come true?" Melissa's voice changed. She shook her head. "You're wrong about that, Reena." She smiled, her eyes shimmering with tears. "Just look around me right now."

The words still rang in Irene's ears when she'd driven back to Lone Pine today, to finish packing and close down the house. Her last stop on the way out of town would be to return the key to the corpulent landlord, who'd be sad to see the two older Taylor women leave after twenty years of paying him rent, not always in cash. Irene had been taping up the last box when the air in the tiny house, with its stained carpets and peeling wallpaper, had suddenly become thick with the haze of neglect and poverty and bad memories. Putting a hand to her throat, she'd run outside, onto the crooked wooden porch to take a staggering breath of cool, clear air.

Now, leaning against the rough wood, Irene stared out at the dark spring night. On the edge of town, between the railroad tracks and the forest, patches of snow still lay on the ground. In the distance, she could see the roof of the tiny house where the Abbotts had once served her cookies after school. Irene pulled her cashmere cardigan a little tighter over her body. She told herself she'd been lucky, really, to have known love, even for such a short time. But if she was lucky, why did it hurt so much?

She'd gotten six different calls from Makhtar since she'd left, all of them from different members of the palace staff who were desperate to have Sharif's wedding to Kalila called off. Well, get in line, she thought. But the latest call had been particularly painful. Aziza had called her at three that morning, waking her up.

"How can I be happy," she'd wailed as greeting, "when both of you are going to be miserable forever?"

"We're not miserable," Irene had lied. "We're fine, and—"

"Fine? You should see my brother right now!"

Irene's throat had ached, and she closed her eyes against the flash of blinding pain. "There's nothing I can do."

"But you said you loved him. How could you love him, and leave him to that woman?"

"He gave me no choice."

"You haven't even called him! Even Basimah

is surprised. She told me, since you didn't call after my wedding was canceled, you must not love Sharif at all."

The knife twisted a little deeper in Irene's heart.

"Aziza," she'd gasped in the dark, empty bed of her condo, "please…"

"No, forget it!" she'd snapped. "Don't even try to save him—just enjoy your life and forget all about us!"

She'd ended the call, leaving Irene weeping for the next three hours in the dark.

She missed Aziza, and Makhtar, and everyone in the palace. But most of all, she missed Sharif. His absence was a hole through her body, leaving everything hollow and devoid of meaning. She felt as if she was dying without him.

Irene's gaze fell on her car.

Her last suitcase had arrived from Makhtar yesterday. It was still in the trunk of her rental car. She hadn't wanted to open it because once she did, the last possible link between her and Sharif would be gone. As long as she didn't open it, she could hope he'd left her some note, some letter to read and treasure for the rest of her life. She'd tried to put it off as long as she could.

She couldn't wait another minute. Grabbing her suitcase from the car, she dragged it up to the porch. With a deep breath, she flung it open.

All she saw were the clothes she'd left behind.

Clothes. Just clothes. Kneeling forward, she started pawing through them more desperately.

Then she saw it.

A note.

With a gasp, she picked it up. She opened it. Her heart pounded as she recognized his jagged handwriting. But the note had only two words: *Unpack thoroughly.*

That was it? She looked at the back. Blank. *That was it?*

Still on her knees, she crushed the note to her chest. All that hope for nothing. She leaned her head against the rough, splinter-covered wood of the porch. She wanted to burst into sobs.

"I heard you were back in town."

Irene looked up through a shimmer of tears to see Carter Linsey standing in front of the ramshackle cottage, wearing a dark vest over a white shirt. Carter, the crush of her teenage years, the supposed heartache that had driven her abroad.

"Carter?" Wiping her eyes, she rose unsteadily to her feet. "What are you doing here?"

"I wanted to see if it was true about you. And it is." He rubbed his jaw, looking her over. "Wow. Your time in Paris really...wow."

Irene looked down at her pearls, sleek cashmere sweater set and slim-fit gray trousers. A little dressy for packing up boxes, but since she hadn't wanted to open that last suitcase, she'd had nothing else clean to wear today. She wore contact lenses instead of glasses now, and she'd probably lost weight, too, since she'd lost her appetite beneath the weight of her grief. She suddenly realized she looked different from the girl who'd left over two years ago. Maybe even fit for the Linsey Mansion, as she'd once dreamed. "Um. Thanks."

"So, your family is really moving, huh?" He tilted his head, his eyes smoldering in the way that had once made her heart beat faster. "It's a shame. Because I was kind of thinking maybe... you'd give me another chance."

She stared at him. "You what?"

"Yes." He ran his hand through his tousled dark blond hair. "I think I made a mistake. About you."

She stared at Carter, wondering how she could have ever thought she loved him. The truth was, she'd never even known him. He'd been just a symbol to her. A way of getting out of an unhappy life.

"Oh, Carter. I'm afraid...I must decline your kind offer."

He blinked. "I thought you had a thing for me."

She gave a low laugh. "I thought so once, too." She looked away. "I thought if I could get a man like you to love me, it would mean I was worth something. But that's not love."

"Then what is?"

"It's not about trying to feel better about yourself," she said slowly. "Love is about *protecting the other person.*" Her throat went dry. "It's about doing everything you can to give the person you love the life they deserve…" Irene's voice trailed off as she remembered how Sharif had done exactly that.

And she'd left him. In that woman's clutches.

But there was nothing I could have done! She told herself desperately. It wasn't as if she had any kind of control over Kalila—or way to stop her from—

The emir is getting what he deserves. Basimah's voice came back to her. *If I could do something to prevent his wedding, if I knew something that would prevent it, I still wouldn't lift a finger.*

Irene stared off in the distance, her lips parted. Basimah had said that long ago, but she'd been too distracted with her own jealousy and misery to pay attention to the words. How had she missed it? How had she not heard?

Even Basimah is surprised, Aziza had said. *She told me, since you didn't call after my wedding was canceled, you must not love Sharif at all.*

"Irene?"

She focused abruptly on Carter's handsome, pouting face.

"Excuse me," she said. "I need to make a phone call. Thanks for stopping by."

"You're—throwing me out?" he said incredulously.

"I'm wishing you all the best. But not with me. Sorry. I'm in love with someone. And he needs me now."

Scratching his head, Carter threw her one last sorrowful, disgruntled look and left. But Irene had already turned away to dial a number in her phone.

"I was wondering why you didn't ask me about it days ago," Basimah said sourly a few minutes later. "I all but told you everything. After he set my lamb free, canceling her wedding, I expected you would ask. But you didn't, you just left, and I decided you must not have loved him as much as I thought. Although abandoning him to that Al-Bahar woman seemed cold…"

"Tell me everything," Irene begged, kicking herself. She listened to Basimah's story, and her heart was suddenly in her throat.

"Go to Sharif. Tell him everything!"

"Me? Get involved in a palace scandal? No. I keep my head down. And so does my sister. That's how we've kept our jobs so long."

"Tell Aziza, then. She can go to her brother and—"

"I'm not having her involved, either. Poor lamb has suffered enough. And she has enough to think about, applying to colleges and preparing to face the big wide world. No. You love him, you save him yourself."

"But he'll never accept this without proof."

"So get it."

Irene wetted her lips. "That would take money. More money than I can even imagine. If he's been blackmailing her for so long, he'll never let that go for cheap. Even if I gave him every penny I have left, he'd just laugh—"

"Do what you want. I'm out of it, and so is my sister, and so is Aziza. It's your problem now," Basimah said simply, and hung up.

Clutching her phone, Irene sank to the rough wood floor of the porch in despair. She'd just been handed the key to everything. But it was too late. It came down to a problem of money. And time. The wedding was in two days, half a world away.

If only she'd kept that diamond necklace Sharif had tried to give her in Italy, she suddenly thought. She gave a half-hysterical laugh. She hadn't realized then she was throwing away her future. And worse: his.

If you don't want the necklace, toss it in the lake. Bury it in the garden. I care not. It's yours. I won't take it back.

But he had. She'd forced him to take it back, pressed it in his hands, and he'd never had another chance to...

Unpack thoroughly.

Irene sat up straight, covering her mouth with her hand. Wide-eyed, she stared across the porch at her open suitcase.

With a gasp, she flung herself toward it.

The day Sharif had dreaded for half his life had come at last. Today was his wedding day.

He was almost glad to get it over with.

In his finest royal robes, of shining white, Sharif walked down the hallway toward the throne room where he would sign his life away.

As was traditional in Makhtar, the bride herself would not be there for the formal signing ceremony. For that small favor, he was glad. He'd already endured enough of Kalila's company this week. Today would be simple and private. All he had to do was go to the throne room where he and the bride's father would sign the papers and conclude the legal formalities, in front of a few witnesses.

So perhaps, if he closed his eyes very tight, he could pretend it was someone else he was marrying today. Someone bright and beautiful, soft and loving.

Against his will, he pictured Irene, with the warmth of a smile glowing in her eyes.

Sharif's footsteps faltered against the marble floor of the hallway, then stopped. He closed his eyes, hearing the roar of blood in his ears. In this moment, he would have given thirty years of his life—forty—if, instead of a billionaire emir who ruled a wealthy nation, he could just be a common goat farmer of the far south, barely able to feed his family each month on a pittance, if only he could have the most basic freedom of all: being with the woman he loved.

"Sire?"

He saw Hassan in front of him.

Sharif tried to speak, had to clear his throat. "Yes?"

"Your bride's father is awaiting you in the throne room, along with the officiant and the witnesses."

Time to face the blade. "I would like you to witness as well."

The man bowed his head. "I am honored." His voice was stilted. He lifted his head with pleading eyes. "But it is not too late…"

"It's nineteen years too late," Sharif said wearily.

"Miss Taylor…"

"Don't say her name," he ground out. "I don't want to hear it. If she's tried to call again, I don't want to—"

"She's here."

Sharif stared at him. He felt all the blood leave his face. "Here?"

"She showed up ten minutes ago at the palace gate. I did not let her through," Hassan added unhappily. "With your standing order, I had the bodyguards detain her. But I thought—" he bit his lip "—maybe you'd changed your mind and—"

Imagining Irene so close to him now, on the day of his wedding, emotion slashed though Sharif.

"No," he choked out. He put his hand to his forehead. If he saw her face now, today of all days, there was no way he'd be able to go through with this wedding. Promise or no promise, he'd cast honor aside and let his country's fate fly as it would. Let the whole nation risk dissolving into chaos and war, if he could just feel Irene's arms around him again—

"There you are, Your Highness." Sheikh Ahmed Al-Bahar, the former vizier and current governor of Makhtar's eastern region, was standing in the doorway of the throne room. He bared his teeth in a smile. "You are late."

"Yes," Sharif said listlessly. "Forgive me. I am coming now."

The man gave an impatient nod and disappeared back into the throne room. Sharif walked toward it as if walking toward his own execution. Each step was more difficult and required more courage than the one before.

He'd given his word.

He had no choice.

Kalila would be a toxic wife, but perhaps she

would still be a good queen, and good mother. Perhaps she…

No, he couldn't even make himself believe that. His stomach twisted at the thought of his future child being raised by her. It felt wrong, so wrong. He didn't want to raise a child with her. Or even create one with her.

There was only one woman he wanted as his wife. Only one he wanted in his bed. One woman to be the mother of his children. And he would never have her.

"Sharif."

He heard Irene's soft, worried voice behind him, and knew he was dreaming. Clenching his hands at his sides, he closed his eyes, enjoying the dream just for one last moment, before he went into the throne room and gave it up forever.

"Sharif!"

The voice was louder now. He frowned, opening his eyes. And turned around.

Irene stood before him, her beautiful face pale. Her lower lip was chapped as if she'd spent the last day chewing on it. Dark circles were beneath her eyes, as if she hadn't slept in days. But she was smiling. And so were the six bodyguards behind her.

His trusted bodyguards had let her into the palace? Against his express orders?

"I don't understand…" Sharif breathed. His

heart lifted to his throat but he tried to ignore it, to force it down. He couldn't allow this to happen. He couldn't let himself love her. "You can't be here, Irene. You have to go…"

"No." Irene's eyes were glowing. "You can't make me leave you ever again."

Slowly, afraid of making the dream disappear, Sharif lifted his hands to touch Irene's upper arms. He felt the warmth of her through her cotton blouse. She was really here. He shuddered.

"Please," he whispered. "This is killing me. Seeing you today, when I must marry another…"

Kalila's voice came sharp behind him. "What the hell is *she* doing here?"

He turned to see her in the wide hallway, dressed like a beautiful royal Makhtari bride, covered with colorful silks and brocades and literally dripping in jewels.

"What am I doing?" Looking at her, Irene suddenly gave a warm smile. "I'm stopping this wedding." She turned to Sharif. "Kalila Al-Bahar cannot marry you. Because *she is already married.*"

It was a dream. It had to be.

His grip tightened. Then he shook his head. "It is impossible. She would never do such a thing."

But her smile only lifted to a grin. "I knew you wouldn't believe me. So I can prove it."

And she stepped aside to reveal the young, extremely muscular man standing behind her.

Kalila's jaw dropped. A mixture of fear, rage and hatred suddenly emanated from her kohl-lined eyes. "Get out of my palace!"

"No," Irene said, so powerful and calm that Sharif did a double take. "*You* will get out of mine."

With a cry, Kalila rushed toward them, as if she intended to claw Irene's eyes out with the red talons of her henna-covered hands. As Sharif stepped protectively in front of Irene, servants started popping their heads out of doorways. Kalila's father came out of the throne room, his own entourage gathering behind him.

"What is going on?" he demanded. He looked at his daughter. "Kalila...?"

But she was looking only at the muscle-bound man. "Don't say it, you piece of trash. Don't even *think* of—"

"Sorry, babe," the man said with a shrug. "She had a better offer."

Sharif whirled to face Irene.

"Tell me," he said urgently.

"Five years ago, in New York, Kalila married her *personal trainer.*" Triumphantly, she held up a piece of paper. "I have the marriage license to prove it."

With a shriek, Kalila tried to reach for it, but

Sharif was faster. Grabbing it from Irene's hand, he looked it over. Then silently handed it to Ahmed Al-Bahar.

The man read, and his face turned scarlet.

"It's a lie—all a trick—" Kalila gasped. "I would never throw my life away on a *servant*—"

"Letters in her own hand." Irene held up a stack of envelopes, bound together with a black ribbon. "Love letters. Notes she sent with the blackmail money, begging him to come back to her."

"Women always fall in love with me," the personal trainer said with a smirk. He shrugged. "I can't help it if she let me take advantage…"

"Dirty blackmailer!" she screamed.

"Lying bigamist," he retorted.

"Aah!" She turned to Irene with murder in her eyes. "And you—how did you know? Who talked?"

"Yes," Sharif breathed. He looked down at Irene. "How did you do this?"

"Let's just say I have my sources." She smiled at him, tears of happiness glistening in her eyes. "I knew you wouldn't believe me without proof. So I bribed Rafael with the diamond necklace you'd hidden behind the liner of my suitcase."

"The necklace?" he echoed.

She lifted an eyebrow. "You said it was mine to do with as I pleased. And I found what I wanted to do with it." Reaching up, she stroked his cheek as tears now streaked down her face. "I wanted to save the life of the man that I loved."

A lump rose in his throat. It was true. She'd saved him.

He took a deep, shuddering breath.

"Does this mean," he whispered, "that you will marry me?"

With a horrendous shriek, Kalila collapsed in her wedding dress in a dead faint.

"Your Highness," her father said behind him, "my daughter has dishonored us. And if not for her—" he glared at Irene "—the dishonor would have been greater." He bowed his head, even as his whole body was tense. "I will deal with Kalila later. For now, I await your punishment."

Silence fell.

"My punishment," Sharif said, "is that you will take her away to live in peace far, far from Makhtar City. And in return—I will say nothing of her betrayal when I announce my change in wedding plans."

The man slowly straightened. His wrinkled face was filled with awe. "You will say nothing of our shame?"

Sharif nodded. "I will say the reason for my change of bride is a personal matter. I will say it's because I've fallen in love for the first time in my life, and there's only one woman I want to be my partner on the throne. Only one woman fated to be my wife. Only one I want to be the mother of my children. I will give this explanation to our people today, but only on one condition." He looked at Irene. "If you agree to marry me right now."

"Say yes," the older man gasped.

"Say yes," Aziza cried from a short distance down the hall.

"Say yes!" cried Basimah and Hassan and all the rest of the palace servants who'd gathered to watch from the ends of the hall.

Irene looked at him, her beautiful pink-cheeked face shining with love.

"Yes," she whispered.

It was the single sweetest word Sharif had ever heard. As he pulled her into his arms, he dimly heard the servants and courtiers burst into spontaneous applause and cries of approval. But all he could think about was the moment his lips would touch hers.

And then...they did.

"Feel married yet?"

Sharif's voice from the bedroom of their Denver hotel suite was equal parts wry and frustrated. Irene smiled at herself in the bathroom mirror. She couldn't blame him for feeling a little impatient. They'd been officially married in Makhtar two days ago, but had yet to have a wedding night.

It had been a hasty, very formal ceremony. Since

she had no official father or male representative, Sharif had abruptly changed the law and decreed that from now on, the marriages would be signed and arranged only by the bride and groom themselves. They'd signed the contracts, then before they'd even had a chance to kiss, the two of them had been forced to part for a full day of wedding celebrations, with the traditional separate feasts for women and men. Irene hadn't been thrilled about attending any six-hour party without Sharif at her side. But as the new sheikha of the land, she'd done it anyway.

Her first royal obligation hadn't been all bad. The women at the feast had come up to her, some shyly, some happily, but all of them relieved to have Irene as the new queen in Kalila's place, even—perhaps especially—the heiress's cousins and distant relatives. Irene was truly touched by their kind words and gracious welcome. Of course, Aziza was over the moon about it, bouncing with joy she didn't even try to disguise. Privately, Irene had thanked Basimah with tears in her eyes. Basimah had demanded that she never mention it again, but then sniffed and wiped her eyes and said she hoped Irene would be a good ruler, loyal and kind.

Irene had still been in shock. She, a nobody from Colorado, the girl who had been mocked and tormented through school about her poverty and family's scandalous past, was now the honored queen of one of the wealthiest nations in the world. She just wished her family could be here to see it…

Her family.

The instant Sharif had arrived at the women's feast to give the groom's traditional greeting, she'd grabbed his arm. "We need to go to Colorado right away," she'd said anxiously. "My sister and mother missed the wedding. They need to be part of it, too…"

"I'll send my plane and bring them here," he growled. He'd stroked her cheek. "I want you in my bed tonight. *Right now…*"

She'd trembled from his touch but remained stubborn. "My mother can't leave Colorado, she's just started rehab. But she might be able to leave for just an hour or two and meet us for a quick ceremony in Denver. Please, Sharif," she'd whispered. "Please."

He'd looked mutinous, then sighed. "Of course, your family must be part of it."

"And," she said thoughtfully, "I could maybe invite Emma—and Cesare…"

An hour later, they were on Sharif's private jet, heading for Colorado. Irene would have been more than willing to have their wedding night at cruising altitude, to join the Mile High Club on their way to Denver, which was nicknamed the Mile

High City. But this time Sharif was the one to grumpily refuse.

"You haven't waited all your life for your wedding night, to have it haphazardly on some random plane." He'd kissed her, and said softly, "We'll have only one first time, you and I, and it's going to be done properly. In a honeymoon suite at the best hotel in the city, after your family has seen us well and truly married." He'd sat down on the white leather sofa, looking very pained as he muttered under his breath, "Even if it kills me."

Emma and Cesare had flown in with their baby at the last minute, joining Irene's mother and sister, who all had happily cried as they watched Sharif and Irene quietly get married again in Denver, in the privacy of a judge's chambers downtown, with no paparazzi and no fuss. Dorothy and Bill Abbott would have approved, Irene had thought with tears in her eyes.

"So now you know," Cesare had informed Sharif smugly after the ceremony, "how irresistible the right woman can be."

He'd laughed good-naturedly. "Yes." He'd looked down at his new bride. "If I'd met Irene sooner, I'd have gotten married a long time ago."

Now, their family and friends were gone. After the quick ceremony was done, Sharif had heartlessly refused to even allow them even a wedding dinner afterward. "A man only has so much willpower, wife," he'd informed her darkly. "We're going to the hotel."

Now, it was just the two of them. Married. Alone.

Nervously, Irene bit her lip as she looked at herself in the mirror of the marble bathroom of the finest suite in the historic, luxurious Brown Palace Hotel. Her cheeks were rosy after the glasses of champagne the manager had given them upon arrival. Her lips were red from her nervous chewing. Her heart was pounding.

Her sister had slyly given her this lingerie as a wedding gift. Irene had never worn anything like it in her life. The white corset pushed up her full breasts, barely covering her nipples, making her waist tiny. She had tiny white lace panties, partially covered with a naughty white garter belt that held up thigh-high white stockings and white satin kitten heels.

"Modest *and* naughty," her sister had chortled with glee. "Perfect for you, Reena!"

Yes, it was. And she could hardly believe she was about ready to leave this bathroom and let Sharif see her in it. But he was her husband now. Her husband, who would know every part of her, as she would know every part of him, for the rest of their lives.

"Irene?" Sharif called hoarsely from the adjoining bedroom.

"Almost ready." Hair up or down? Her hands shook as she held up her dark hair. Then she let the dark waves tumble over her bare shoulders. Her legs were trembling as she went out into the bedroom of the enormous, elegant hotel suite.

Sharif was stretched out across the enormous four-poster bed, still wearing the black suit from their ceremony. He turned toward her, smiling. "Finally—"

His voice choked off when he saw her in the white corset and garter belt. He sat up, his expression pale.

Irene faltered. "Do you not like it?"

"Like it?" he said hoarsely.

Never taking his eyes off her, Sharif rose unsteadily to his feet and walked to where she stood trembling on the blue carpet. For a moment, he just looked down at her with his dark eyes, the infinitely deep gaze that saw every part of her and loved her in spite of her flaws, as she loved him in spite of his. He cupped her face.

"I nearly died just looking at you. I nearly had a heart attack. If I didn't know you were mine…"

"But you do," she said as her heart started beating again. She smiled at him. "Yours now. Yours forever."

"I love you, Irene, my beautiful wife. I will love you until I die."

She put her hand over his. "You're trembling."

Sharif's lips lifted into a crooked smile. "Sorry."
He took a deep breath. "But you see, in a way, it's
my first time, too..."

She licked her lips. Then, lifting on tiptoe in
the white heels, she kissed him very, very softly
on the lips, then whispered five words in his ear.

"Take me," she said. "Take me now."

Her husband kissed her hungrily, savagely, and
lifted her in his arms. Never breaking the kiss,
he carried her to their wedding bed, and there,
they shared their private, final vow, the one she'd
waited for all her life, in the sweet promise without words that would last not just tonight, not just
tomorrow, but forever.

* * * * *